Sea Girls

The Crystal City

SeaGirls

The Crystal City

g.g. elliot

Piccadilly Press • London

First published in Great Britain in 2006
by Piccadilly Press Ltd,
5 Castle Road, London NW1 8PR
www.piccadillypress.co.uk

A catalogue record for this book is available from the British Library

ISBN: 1 85340 878 6 (trade paperback)
ISBN-13: 9 781853 408786

1 3 5 7 9 10 8 6 4 2

Printed and bound in Great Britain by Bookmarque Ltd.
Typeset by Textype, Cambridge
Set in ACaslon and Present
Cover design by Fielding Design
Illustration by Sue Hellard

Papers used by Piccadilly Press are produced from
forests grown and managed as a renewable resource,
and which conform to the requirements of recognised forestry
accreditation schemes.

Chapter 1

POLLY CLIMBED TO THE top diving board and paused for a moment. She then walked to the very edge and looked down at all the people surrounding the flat, still water below. Calmly, she bounced twice and launched herself high above the swimming pool. Unlike the girls before her, she made it look so easy, twisting and somersaulting in the air, then dropping like a gannet and entering the water with hardly a splash. While the audience was busy clapping, she swam to the other end of the pool without surfacing. To all who had watched, the whole sequence had seemed perfectly straightforward and perfectly brilliant. When Polly eventually climbed out of the water at the other end, however, she was feeling extremely agitated. In that short space of time, something had happened which would affect her life for ever.

As she had dived into the pool, the water had gone straight up her nose. Usually this would have made her choke and rush to the surface, gasping for air, but, much to her amazement, she had carried on sucking in water through her nose and blowing it out through her mouth. It was as if a passageway had cleared in her head. She could breathe underwater!

When she surfaced, stunned, part of her wanted to tell everybody, but something made her stop. For the moment, she felt she must keep this incredible discovery to herself.

Since she was a baby, Polly Jenkins had always loved water and anything to do with it. Bath-time had been her absolute favourite and, according to her mother, she would try to swim even in the shallow bath. She was swimming proficiently by the time she was three and when, later, the school realised her gift, they made special adjustments to her timetable so she could swim every day. Her father was always joking about it; he reckoned that if she didn't swim regularly, she'd probably dry out like an old dishcloth!

But Polly had never been an ordinary child. Her history was unusual to say the least. Fourteen years ago the papers had reported a tiny baby being found at Trader's Cove – a mile outside the seaside town of Eastleigh, where she lived now. An old lady, who had been walking her dog on a cold, clear morning, had come across a baby, naked apart from thick seaweed wrapped tightly round her little body. The ambulance men and the doctors at the local hospital had marvelled that the tiny mite hadn't died from exposure, but apart from being a little hungry, she was in remarkably fine condition.

Polly had often wondered about her real parents and why they had deserted her and risked her life. But she loved her adoptive parents, and knew they loved her, so she didn't dwell on this much.

As she towelled herself dry in the changing room, Polly thought back to what she'd noticed only a couple of months ago in the bathroom mirror, and shivered slightly. She had realised that her body was beginning to take the shape of many of the female swimmers she'd seen on television: narrow hips, flat stomach and strong, powerful shoulders. She remembered hoping her shoulders didn't become any broader, as she thought this would look a bit unfeminine. She'd also wished she was slightly more blessed in the breast area, but decided she wasn't going to worry about that yet. And she hadn't liked her rather large feet, which, though excellent for pushing her through the water, could never be thought of as attractive.

She'd been just about to put her clothes back on,

when she'd happened to turn and glimpse her back in the mirror. For the first time ever she'd noticed a tiny blue-black mark in the middle of her lower back. She couldn't see it very well, but being aware of all the fuss there had been lately about moles and skin cancer, she'd taken her dad's shaving mirror – which magnified – to have a closer look. To her surprise, the mark was in the shape of a fish. She'd shown it to her mother, who'd told her that she'd always had it and it was nothing to worry about. In quiet moments, however, Polly had often found herself thinking about it.

Dressed now, Polly managed to shrug off this memory, and her latest discovery that she could breathe under-water, as she joined her team-mates to celebrate.

'Polly, darling, have you got everything? We really should be off.'

'Won't be long, Mum. I'm just texting Kirsty. Her dad's got the directions.'

It was Saturday morning, a few weeks after the diving display, and Polly and her mother were heading for the finals of the inter-county schools girls' swimming gala. Polly's school stood more than a fair chance of winning, mainly due to her. She was quite the most remarkable young swimmer they had ever had and she'd never been beaten in any competition. Although only in Year Ten, she'd been asked to coach the whole team – even the sixth formers – as she was by far the best. She had helped them realise that technique was vital – it was crucial to get your stroke and breathing absolutely right. You only had to look at all the trophies and cups in the glass cabinets in the school hall to see what an effect she'd had.

The swimming races went well for Polly's school. Polly, as expected, won her heats – in breaststroke and backstroke – easily, and all that remained was the four-by-two hundred metres relay. There was another team – Sunborough High, from the north coast – who were also doing rather well; so well that whichever team came first in the relay would win the whole match.

Polly kept hearing the other competitors talking about a girl from Sunborough High who also had a reputation for winning every swimming competition she went in for, and had won the freestyle and butterfly races by a long way. She'd been put on the last leg of the relay – the freestyle – against Polly.

When this girl was pointed out to her, Polly couldn't help noticing that she looked similar to herself. She too was tall and slim with wide shoulders and, to Polly's satisfaction, big feet.

The relay began. The first swimmers were fairly evenly matched and stayed within a couple of metres of each other. When Polly began her leg, her school, Eastleigh, was just in the lead, and she fully expected to increase this lead by a long way. However, as she finished her first length, she realised that the girl from Sunborough was very close to her. She decided she must make more of an effort and cannoned down the next length, but the other girl was still tailing her, much to her annoyance. Polly gritted her teeth and on the turn set off down the third length determined to break away from her. By this time, they had left all the other swimmers well behind.

As they turned for the last length, they were neck and neck and Polly was getting nervous. This was the first time she had ever had to really push herself in a competition. As she thrashed along, she could hear the near hysterical screaming of the spectators round the pool. With all her remaining strength she kicked harder, and at last it seemed her rival was beginning to drop behind. But when Polly was about fifteen metres from the end and victory, she saw from the corner of her eye that the other girl had caught her up. She could do nothing about it – her mystery rival won by a hair's breadth. The other swimmers were about a length and a half behind them.

Polly's team-mates clustered round their captain.

'What's up, Poll?' asked Kirsty Douglas. 'Are you feeling OK? What happened?'

'I thought I was winning. But she just wouldn't give in.'

'You didn't *let* her win, did you?' asked Naomi Blunt, who couldn't believe her hero had been beaten.

'Oh yeah, sure,' replied Polly tetchily. 'Why would I do that? Of course I didn't.'

'Sorry. It's just that *we* can't get anywhere near you even when you're not trying,' said Naomi.

Polly would have preferred to avoid the presentation, but realised it would be unsportsmanlike not to attend. A girl from a school in Exeter stepped on to the third-place podium and Polly took the second-place one. The winner then hopped up between the two of them, beaming. Polly couldn't help noticing the girl had bright, sea-green eyes just like hers. She leaned over to shake hands with Polly and then turned to the other girl. As she was doing so, Polly saw her back and stared. Then she nearly fell off the podium as her head began to spin. She blinked a couple of times, shook her head to try and clear it, and then stared again. There, right in the middle of the girl's back, was a mark identical to hers – a tiny, blue-black fish!

Chapter 2

POLLY STAYED IN THE changing room until all the
other girls had gone. She couldn't understand what had
just happened. She'd been beaten at the only thing she
did well, by someone who turned out to have exactly
the same strange birthmark as her. She dressed absent-
mindedly then went up to the café for a drink. There
she saw the girl sitting at a table by herself, eating a
doughnut. Polly knew she had to talk to her.

'Hi,' Polly said as cheerily as she could muster. 'Well
done. You were pretty awesome. Do you mind if I join
you?'

The girl smiled. 'Oh hi! Yeah, pull up a chair. You
were good too. I thought you were going to beat me
right up to the last bit.'

'So did I. I've never been beaten before – ever. Sorry,
does that sound a bit show-offy?'

The other girl laughed. 'No – I'd have felt the same. I've never been beaten either. In fact, you're the only person who's ever come close. It was a real shock, I can tell you.'

They grinned at each other and the ice was broken. After that, Polly and the girl chatted away about competitions and schools and where they lived. Polly found she really liked her, which was quite unusual. Although well liked herself, Polly had always found it difficult to get really close to anyone. This girl seemed different somehow – Polly felt as if she'd known her for ages. After a while, she plucked up the courage to ask about the tiny mark on her back. The girl looked surprised.

'Oh that! I noticed it a year or so ago,' she said, slightly self-consciously. 'It's just a sort of birthmark. Why?'

Polly hesitated, peered quickly round the empty café and then said quietly, 'You're never going to believe this, but I've got one in the same place.'

'You're kidding. What's yours like?'

'It's the same – like a tiny fish. Do you want to see?' Polly looked round again to make absolutely sure no one was watching and then she lifted her tracksuit top to show the other girl. Then they sat, deep in thought, staring at each other.

'What's your name?' the girl asked eventually.

'Polly. Polly Jenkins. Yours?'

'Lisa Roberts. Hey, look, pleased to meet you – I think!' She laughed to make sure Polly realised it was a joke. 'Are your mum and dad here?'

'Only Mum. Dad had to work. He's got a small garage and couldn't get away – Saturday's his busy day, see. What about yours?'

'My mum'll be here in a bit.'

Polly's mum arrived with Lisa's. 'Everything all right?' Polly's mum asked innocently.

'Erm, yeah, Mum,' replied Polly. 'Apart from being beaten by Lisa here! We were just talking.'

'Oh, well done, Lisa! I was just telling your mum that you're the first person to outswim Polly – it was an amazing race. Polly, darling, are you ready to go?'

'Could you give us ten minutes?'

'Sure, darling – I could do with a cup of tea myself.' And she went off to get one with Lisa's mum.

Polly turned to Lisa as soon as they were out of range. 'Hey, this mark thing is very odd, isn't it? Do you think we ought to tell anyone?'

'Tell anyone what? I think it's weird, and you think it's weird . . . but you know what they'll say: it's just an odd coincidence – we both love swimming and we've both got similar fish birthmarks. So what?'

'I wonder if there are kids all over the place with fish marks,' said Polly.

'How would we know, unless we go around pulling

their shirts off. We could get arrested for that.'

Polly laughed. 'Hey, what's your mobile number?'

She put it on her phone and Lisa did the same with Polly's.

'It's weird, considering I've only know you for ten minutes, but I feel I've known you for ages,' said Polly.

Lisa smiled warmly. 'I feel the same,' she said.

Chapter 3

OVER THE NEXT COUPLE of weeks Polly and Lisa spoke a lot. They found they could chat away really easily about anything and everything. It was on their fourth phone conversation that Lisa happened to mention that she'd been adopted.

Polly felt a strange tingle come over her. 'Adopted?' she managed to gasp.

'Yeah! So what?'

'S-so was I,' she stuttered.

Lisa was silent for several seconds. 'You're not . . . you're taking the mickey, aren't you?'

'No, honest. I was abandoned as a baby.'

'You were what?' Lisa almost shouted.

'I was left on a beach close to where I live now. Why?'

Polly couldn't see, of course, but Lisa had gone pale.

'Are you all right?' said Polly. 'What is it?'

'So was I,' Lisa replied, in a small voice. 'I was found on Marlborough Beach, just a few miles up the coast. How weird is that?'

The two girls fell totally silent, trying to grasp the meaning of what they'd just found out.

Polly broke the silence finally. 'I wonder what the chances are of two girls, of a similar age, with the same birthmark, who both love swimming, being abandoned on a beach in the West Country? What's it all about? Is there anyone else like us? What does it mean?'

'I reckon it's worth trying to find out.'

'But how?'

'Can you get on the Internet easily? I'm usually pretty good at finding out stuff. We could both have a go.'

As soon as she was off the phone, Polly went to the family computer. She typed 'abandoned children' into Google, but all it came back with were numerous charities seeking homes or sponsors for homeless children in places like Africa or South America. She typed in various combinations of words and eventually, on one research website, she discovered that between five and fifteen years ago, there had been a small rise in the number of children found abandoned in Britain, and that there was a corresponding rise in the number of mothers who had never been traced.

Then she phoned Lisa back and told her what she'd found.

'I'm ahead of you,' Lisa replied. 'I found that site a couple of hours ago, and at the bottom it said you could e-mail questions. I've just got their reply.'

'What was your question?' asked Polly excitedly.

'I wanted to know if they could tell me where the babies were found. You know, where in Britain.'

'And?'

'For some reason, they said, there seemed to be more in the south-west, particularly in Devon and Cornwall.'

A few weeks later, at the beginning of the summer holidays, Polly asked her parents if it would be all right for her new best friend to come and stay. There was one thing that she had to tell Lisa in person, and for some reason she just knew it was more important than anything else. She had to tell Lisa that she could breathe underwater . . .

It was a beautiful day when Lisa reached Polly's, so the two girls decided to go for a swim at Trader's Beach, the place where Polly had been found fourteen years earlier. Polly borrowed her mum's bike and lent Lisa hers.

After the hot cycle to the beach, the two girls locked their bikes and straightaway stripped to their costumes, ran down to the beach and flopped into the cool, sparkly waves. It was the first time they had swum together since the area finals, and for two girls obsessed with water it was the best thing in the world. They played in the shallows and tumbled around in the surf. A large wave knocked Lisa off her feet and pushed her to the bottom. She came up spluttering.

'Steady,' laughed Polly, 'don't drink it all, we'll need some to swim in.'

'Flipping thing caught me off balance. Hey, how long can you stay underwater? I bet I can beat you.'

Polly hesitated. 'Quite a long time, I reckon. I've never really tried.' She knew she had told a fib, but the question had taken her by surprise. She realised that now was the time to tell her new friend her biggest secret.

Polly dived to the bottom and began by letting a stream of bubbles flow from her mouth. She then closed her mouth and breathed in the water through her nose and forced it out through her mouth and ears. Lisa, who'd been staring down from above, was astonished and horrified when the bubbles stopped and Polly did not come up for air. Staring harder, she noticed that Polly appeared to be smiling up at her from a metre or so underwater. Polly then lay on her back on the bottom, put her hands behind her head and pretended to go to sleep.

In a panic, Lisa dived down and dragged her friend to the surface, shaking her as she did so.

'What on earth are you up to – are you completely and totally mad? Have you lost the will to live or something? You'll drown yourself!'

'Sorry,' said Polly with a little giggle. 'It's just something I found I could do – breathe underwater!'

'Don't be daft – that's impossible. Look, how did you do what you just did?'

'I'm not sure. I only discovered I could quite recently.'

Then Polly told Lisa all about the diving display and suddenly being able to breathe underwater. She told her how weird it had made her feel to have such an unusual secret and how difficult it had been to keep it to herself. She felt very relieved telling Lisa, and hoped she'd understand. Polly glanced nervously at her friend, waiting for a reaction.

Lisa looked serious and a little frightened. 'You don't . . . you don't think it's anything to do with . . . you know, everything else?'

'What, us being the best swimmers, and abandoned and the mark and everything? I don't know. Hey, why don't you have a go?'

'I'm beginning to wish I'd never met you, Polly! You don't often come across people who tell you to stick your head underwater and breathe in, the first opportunity they have!' With that Lisa grinned and ducked down, but as soon as the water went up her nose she panicked and spluttered to the surface.

'I nearly drowned!' she gasped. 'Are you mad or am I madder?'

'Try and stay cool,' said Polly. 'Take it nice and easy, like I did.'

'Oh yeah – and then drown quietly, eh? I'm full of tricks like that.'

She tried again – and then again. It still didn't work and by now she had swallowed so much water that she was beginning to get cross.

'OK', said Polly, 'maybe you *shouldn't* take it easy. Breathe in the water suddenly, as hard as you can. It might just need a push.'

Lisa tried a couple of times, but came up spluttering as before.

On the third try, however, she felt a strange click in her head, just behind her nose. To Polly's relief and delight, she began to grin underwater. Polly dived down to join her and they hugged, shook hands and stuck their tongues out at each other. When they came up to the surface, Lisa was ecstatic.

'I just don't believe it. Did you see me? I was really doing it! It's so cool.'

'I know,' said Polly, in a rather more subdued voice. 'I've wanted to tell you about it for ages, but I knew you wouldn't believe me until I could prove it.'

The two friends dived below the surface and set off for the deeper water. They loved the sensation of being free from the need to fill their lungs every minute or so, and as they dived into the cool, green depths, swimming in and out of shoals of tiny green and silver fish, the full implications of all the similarities between them began to dawn. Despite the water becoming colder as they went deeper and deeper, neither of them seemed to feel it. They now knew for sure that they were linked by something more than coincidence.

When they got back to the beach they sat silently, drying in the late afternoon sunshine, both deep in their own thoughts.

Lisa broke the silence and spoke slowly and deliberately. 'I'm beginning to get a bit scared. It's as if we're not proper humans – like we're from a different planet.'

'I know,' said Polly. 'I was really freaking out before I met you. It's as if a whole part of me belongs somewhere else, like . . .'

'Underwater!' Lisa giggled.

'I thought the only things that could breathe underwater were fish and frogs and things. We did it in biology last term. Miss Grayson, our biology teacher, told us they've got these things that mean they can get the oxygen out of the water.'

'Was that what we were doing? It felt as if the water was leaving through my ears. Is that possible?'

Lisa was silent for another minute, then spoke again. 'When we were underwater, I kept thinking that that was the real world and that the beach and the rest of the land was just somewhere you come to visit, but don't stay for long. Do you know what I mean or is it just me?'

'Yes, I do. Where *do* you think we come from?' asked Polly, with an intense expression on her face. 'It's got something to do with being found on beaches, I reckon, but I don't know what. It's almost too scary to think about. I'm not sure I like the idea of being half fish and half frog or something! It's not exactly sexy, is it?'

'I don't know. Imagine fancying a frog! There are princesses who kiss frogs, aren't there?'

Polly giggled. 'You know what I mean, stupid.'

Polly and Lisa talked and talked and talked for the rest of her stay.

On her last day they were just discussing when they could next meet up when Lisa said, 'Hey, by the way, I want to go to Cornwall next week.'

'To the surf championships?' asked Polly.

'Yeah, I reckon they'll be awesome. I wonder if Matt Miller will win again. He's so cool.'

'I think he's brilliant too.'

'Great minds,' said Lisa, jumping to her feet in excitement. 'Let's both go! Would your mum and dad let you?'

'I shouldn't think so – not if it's just us two. Not unless there was some grown-up involved.'

'Consider it sorted. My gran lives close to where it's being held. We could stay with her.'

Chapter 4

POLLY AND LISA WERE really excited about going to the National Surfing Championships at Newquay. They both enjoyed body-boarding themselves, and they were both massive fans of Matt Miller.

Matt Miller was the boy wonder of the British surfing world. At just fourteen, he'd won every junior championship possible and now, three years later, he had entered the adult competition. He was tall and tanned, with long, straggly hair bleached almost white by the sun and sea, and bright green eyes which seemed almost luminous framed by his brown face.

Lisa's gran was delighted to have the two girls to stay for the week. She drove them to the beach each morning and picked them up after the last event in the afternoon. On the final day of the competition, the waves were at their best – not particularly high, but long and unbroken and toppling over in continuous lines. Eager surfing fans from all over the country crowded the beach as they cheered on their favourite competitors. By the final event, Matt Miller was well ahead of the others, even though some of his rivals were much older than him.

His very last run left no doubt in anyone's mind – including the judges' – that he was by far and away the finest surfer present – a complete natural. The crowd on the beach watched in awe as he wove in and out of the foaming peaks and deep troughs, leaping from one end of the board to the other, swivelling backwards and forwards and ducking down into the tubes formed by the curling waves. It was as if he were part of the very wave itself. At the end of his last run and with an almost perfect score, he coasted in on the remains of a spent wave and gave his adoring public a theatrical bow.

'Oh my God, he's *so* awesome and *so* fit,' cried Lisa. 'I've just got to talk to him. It's probably the only chance I'll ever get.'

'Hmm. He's not my type,' replied Polly, who usually preferred the more clean-cut, boy-band look, 'but I know what you mean. He *is* fit. What are you going to say to him?'

'I'll ask him to swim away with me into the sunset.'

'I bet you don't,' said Polly with a laugh.

'He was so much better than the rest, wasn't he?

It's as if he's from a different planet. Planet Surf.'

At the mention of a different planet the two girls caught each other's eye.

'You're not thinking what I'm thinking, are you?' asked Polly in a faraway voice.

'Look, you never know. How wicked would it be if he was one of us?'

Polly and Lisa wove their way through the fans and photographers to the front where the cups were being handed out. The sun had now gone in and a stiff breeze was blowing. Most of the other competitors, though still wearing wetsuits and swathed in thick towels, were shivering – but Matt, still in his damp baggy shorts, was completely relaxed, sipping a cold Coke and signing autographs for the fans.

Polly gasped in astonishment at her friend and then pointed to Matt's feet, which were large and flat like theirs. Lisa nodded conspiratorially and, as was her way, went straight up to him and began talking, while Polly casually strolled round behind and examined his back. She was almost surprised that she wasn't more surprised – there on his back was the fish-shaped birthmark. She gave Lisa a surreptitious thumbs-up. So Matt Miller, the young man so perfectly at home on and in the waves, also bore the mark that the girls had come to know so well. Both knew without needing to consult the other that they simply had to ask him about it.

At first he seemed cool and almost conceited: he knew he was something special and expected everyone else to recognise the fact. Lisa realised she was getting nowhere talking fan-talk, so decided to be direct.

'That's a weird mark on your back.'

The young surfer appeared taken aback.

'What mark?'

'The little fish in the middle of your back. My friend, Polly, over there just noticed it.'

'So what?'

'We both have the same one.'

When Matt had managed to extricate himself from the rest of his fans, the three of them found a quiet place to sit and Polly and Lisa showed him their identical marks.

'I only noticed it a while back,' he said. 'I thought it was a bit weird, but then forgot about it. It's no big deal.'

At first Matt reckoned they must have copied his mark in some way. He'd been photographed for quite a few surfing magazines, he told them, so they could have seen it in one of them. When they swore they hadn't, he had to admit that it was so small that it would barely be visible in photos anyway, and that nobody else had ever mentioned it. It was when the girls told him that they had both been abandoned as babies, however, that his voice dropped to a whisper.

'I never knew my real folks either.'

'Were you left on a beach like us?' asked Polly.

'No, I was found on a dinghy, apparently. It was floating in the sea, miles from the shore. My real parents, who everyone thought must have been sailing it, were never found. Nobody was ever reported missing. It was just poor little me, all alone in the ocean. How tragic was that? I was only a few weeks old.'

'Just like us!' said Polly.

'Who adopted you?' asked Lisa.

'A couple from St Agnes – you know, just up the coast. They're called Miller, same as me – obviously.'

'Are they cool?' asked Polly.

'Oh yeah, dead cool. My dad builds boats and just loves everything to do with the sea. I suppose that's why I got in to surfing.'

The three of them chatted easily for a while about surfing and swimming.

'Can you breathe underwater?' Lisa suddenly asked, out of the blue.

Matt looked taken aback and then smiled a superior kind of smile. 'No! 'Course not! Nobody can. What sort of a stupid question's that?' He stood up, as if to walk away.

'We can,' broke in Polly, trying not to sound smug. 'For as long as we want.'

'Are you taking the mickey? It's impossible – unless you're both fish!'

'That's what *we* thought, till we cracked how to do it.'

Matt looked completely dismissive at first but his curiosity was beginning to get the better of him. The girls seemed to be genuine. He sat down again. 'OK, girls. How does it work then?' he asked patronisingly.

Lisa laughed. 'It's all about having the guts to give it a go. Then, just as you think you're about to choke and drown, it all kicks in, honest! We'll show you if you want. It's so cool.'

'We don't think everyone can do it,' said Polly. 'We wonder if it's anything to do with the mark and being abandoned babies and stuff. It's all a bit unnatural. You should try.'

'OK – when?' he asked, half humouring, half challenging them. If he hadn't always felt a bit different to other people, and if he hadn't felt a strange affinity to these two earnest girls, he might not have bothered.

'Whenever you like,' said Polly. 'It'd better be in the next few days, though. We're going home soon.'

Matt thought for a short while. 'Tell you what, I've been lent my dad's boat on Tuesday. Do you guys want a ride? We can get away from any nosey tourists, and then you can show me.'

On Tuesday morning Lisa and Polly set out with Matt Miller in his father's luxurious twin-engined motor-cruiser. It was a beautiful, calm day, with a cloudless sky and hardly a ripple on the blue-green water. The boat flew along, seeming hardly to touch the glassy surface, and the girls laughed at the pure joy of doing something they'd only dreamed of before.

After an hour or so, Matt throttled back and suggested they all went for a swim. He soon realised, though, that he would have to stay with the boat, as it was too deep to use the anchor. So he sat back and watched the two girls plunge into the cool, clear sea.

Fascinated, he followed the lines of bubbles as Polly and Lisa swam deeper and deeper, until they were just vague dark shapes way down below. Eventually they disappeared altogether. After a while, he checked his watch and realised they'd been down for over ten minutes. At first he was excited – no one could hold their breath for that long! What they'd said about breathing underwater must be true!

After they had been gone for fifteen minutes however, Matt became concerned. Concern grew into real worry, as his eyes desperately scoured the surface all around the boat. When they had been down for over half an hour, he panicked, grabbed his mobile and phoned the coastguards. It seemed to him to take ages for the lifeboat to arrive and, by the time it did, Matt was frantic.

Polly and Lisa had dived as deep as possible, just to

prove to Matt that they had told the truth about breathing underwater. When they reached the seabed, they noticed a small cave with a shoal of pink fish disappearing into it. Lisa was inquisitive and swam right up to have a closer look. But as she approached, a strong current began to tug her forwards towards the mouth of the cave. She tried to turn round but found the current too great. Though an exceedingly strong swimmer she was powerless against such a force.

Lisa disappeared right in front of Polly's eyes. Polly naturally thought her friend had gone in of her own accord and swam over to see what she was up to. She was only a few metres from the entrance to the cave when she too was taken up by the strong current and was pulled through after her friend.

Polly found herself being churned over and over, losing any sense of direction. It felt like a much stronger version of the chutes at the water park she had visited the previous summer. She seemed to be spiralling down for ever – though in reality it was only minutes – and then she found herself flying out of the tunnel at the other end.

Polly felt dizzy, confused and very, very frightened. It took some time for her head to clear well enough to take in her new surroundings. She found herself in what seemed to be a completely new ocean, lit by a strange, incandescent glow. It was a gloomy underwater world completely different to the sunlit one she and Lisa had just left. As she looked around her, it was as if she was hovering above the sharp pinnacles of what appeared to be an awesome underwater mountain range with ravines that disappeared into total nothingness way, way down below. It was as if an ancient land had been submerged, way back in time.

But where was Lisa? Polly looked about her anxiously. Just as she was really beginning to panic Lisa tapped her on the shoulder. They hugged each other in relief. By sign language, both made it perfectly clear that neither had any idea where they were or how they could get back. Above them was what appeared to be an impenetrable ceiling of solid rock, apart from the entrance of the tunnel they had just come through, which continued to gush water too powerful to swim against.

Unsure of where to go, Polly and Lisa were soon drifting amongst dense shoals of huge silver fish whose large eyes glowed like torches, illuminating the water in front of them. There were giant green turtle-like creatures, the size of small cars, floating aimlessly through the twilight depths and exquisite jellyfish decked in their gaudiest finery hanging like parachutes in outer space. Everywhere they looked there were creatures they had never seen before – even in books or on TV. If they hadn't been so scared it might have been more enjoyable – this incredible wonderland of towering corals and brilliantly coloured underwater plants, some the size of giant trees.

For nearly an hour they swam backwards and forwards, trying to find a passageway through the ceiling to the ocean above. The girls were desperately holding on to the hope that there was a way back to the land above.

Suddenly, a horror-stricken Polly nudged Lisa and pointed. There, far in the distance, they could just make out three enormous fish. They had both seen pictures of giant sharks and killer whales, but these looked even bigger and even scarier, with huge circular eyes that sent wide beams of bright green light far out in front of them. The girls watched, petrified, as one of the fish approached, opened its vast mouth and swallowed a shoal of what must have contained a hundred of the smaller, pale fish.

The two friends swung round and swam as fast as they could away from the giant fish, but, as they did so, one of the monsters turned and headed their way. It had spotted them! They were no match for its under-water speed. Just as it was nearly upon them, Polly noticed something above the huge green eyes that com-pletely astonished her – it was a symbol of a fish . . . a fish identical to the one on her and her best friend's backs.

Chapter 5

THE TWO GIRLS WERE motionless in the water as if suspended in liquid space. They had heard on TV that at the bottom of the ocean there lived creatures that man had never seen before, but nothing could have prepared them for anything as frightening as this huge silver-green monster. As it loomed closer, they noticed that it didn't swim like a fish, but seemed to be propelled from behind. At once, both girls realised that it wasn't a living creature at all, but an ingenious submarine that was made to look like one. Exhausted and unable to swim any further, at first the girls felt relief: perhaps they weren't going to be eaten up. Through the round windows from which light flooded, they could just make out the silhouettes of human beings who seemed to be driving it. Perhaps they were going to be rescued!

Suddenly they felt a vibration through the water and to their horror, the large jaws right in front of them began to cantilever open. They were going to be swallowed alive! Before they could react in any way, Polly and Lisa felt themselves being sucked in by a force even stronger than the one that had pulled them into the underwater cave. Try as they might, the terrified girls couldn't make any headway against it and soon they were inside, held against a mesh wall, like fish in a net.

They were caught in what appeared to be a large metal hold. The huge jaws began to close slowly and noisily behind them and as they thudded shut, the level of the seawater began to drop as it was pumped out of what looked like a large drainage grill in the bottom of the fish's mouth. After a few minutes, Polly and Lisa found themselves sitting in puddles on the floor of the bare metal room. At least they found they were able to breathe the air.

'Have you ever felt like fish-food?' groaned Lisa, relieved to be able to speak to her friend at last.

'I'm glad you can still joke,' murmured Polly.

They were just wondering what was going to happen next when, at the back of the hold, a door slid to one side and they were nearly blinded by the brilliant light that flooded into their damp, smelly cell. As they peered nervously through the opening, they could just make out a cabin with three men sitting at the controls.

One of them stood up and stepped forward. He was wearing a figure-hugging outfit that looked as if it was made of shimmering fish skin, and shiny rubber boots. He, and the two other men, were tall, with green eyes and blond hair.

Lisa spoke first. 'Where are we?'

The man hesitated, as if trying to work out what language she was speaking. He talked to his fellow crewmen and after a couple of minutes of urgent conversation, he turned to the girls again.

He spoke in a clear, loud, heavily-accented, but not unkind voice. 'Welcome to our ship.'

Polly and Lisa stared at each other. They were relieved that he seemed friendly.

He spoke again. 'Where have you come from?'

'We come from up above,' replied Lisa, bravely. 'We were in a boat on the surface. Can you take us back? Our friend is waiting for us.'

The three men looked at each other in surprise.

'What is this *surface*?' asked the first man, who seemed to be the captain. 'We have no word like that in our country.' His friends looked at each other nervously.

'It's what boats float on. It's at the top of the sea – you know – where the waves are,' Lisa said, growing in confidence.

'The top of the sea, you say?' A small artificial-looking

32

smile played on the captain's lips. 'And what, pray, is above that?'

Lisa looked at him strangely. 'Is he messing us about?' she whispered to Polly.

Polly spoke. 'The whole world is above the sea. All the different countries, planes, birds, everything – they're all above here. You must know that.'

'But the *sea* is everything,' the man said. 'The only life there is. Ever since the great flood, we have been completely engulfed in water.'

The two friends glanced at each other with raised eyebrows. Was this man completely mad?

'You had better come with us,' he said, gently now. 'We will talk later.'

The three men returned to the control room, this time leaving the door to the hold open. At the captain's signal to the man at the controls, the boat made a loud whirring noise, shuddered slightly and began to dive at such a rate that Polly and Lisa were forced to grab on to anything they could find to stay on their feet. 'Where are you taking us?' demanded Lisa in a shrill voice that revealed a mixture of fear and anger.

'We are taking you to Fortuna. You will be safe with us.'

'We don't want to be safe with you, thank you very much,' cried Lisa, more bravely now. 'We want to go home. There's someone waiting for us up above.'

The three men ignored her as their ship increased in speed. As they peered through the tiny portholes, Polly and Lisa could see the subterranean world flying past. Down and down they went for what seemed for ever. Their ears buzzed with the increasing pressure. Just as the ship began to slow down Polly called to Lisa and pointed. 'What on earth is that?'

Ahead of them, only just visible through the deep murky water, and stretching in all directions, was what looked like a huge crystal dome, bigger than anything they had ever seen, with plumes of bubbles issuing from a forest of tall chimneys on its surface. From inside the dome there came a strange glow, which lit up the surrounding water. Around the outside of the dome, they could just make out the remains of what appeared to be ancient buildings and the skeletons of petrified trees. All seemed to be smothered in a thick layer of silt, as if they had lain there for hundreds of years.

'That, my friends,' the captain said, pointing to the dome, 'is the ancient land of Fortuna, where we come from. We are fishermen who provide food for our people.'

The submarine glided straight for the nearest part of the dome and as it did so the girls could just make out that it was constructed from millions of glass panels that were so thick that they could hardly see anything inside.

Near the bottom edge of the dome was a bulge the size of a large building, which their boat seemed to be heading towards. Through the front window, illuminated by the searchlights, they saw that huge doors were beginning to slide open as they approached. The submarine edged through the gap extremely cautiously and came to rest on what appeared to be an oversized table, next to another identical craft. Then the massive doors closed behind them and the water-level dropped as seawater was pumped out, rather like what had happened earlier in the fishing hold.

Fifteen minutes later, the craft was high and dry. Then the jaws of the boat opened in front of the girls again, to reveal a narrow, moving pavement.

The girls stared in pure bewilderment. Never in their lives had they seen anything like this, even in the movies.

'That conveyor-belt thing must be to take the fish,' said Polly, when she finally found her voice.

'I think we *are* the fish,' muttered Lisa, who despite everything had just managed to hang on to her sense of humour.

'What are they going to do with us?'

Despite her bravado, Lisa looked worried. 'We'll soon find out. They're asking us to go with them.'

The captain and his men were getting on the moving path and gesturing for the girls to follow.

Chapter 6

AHEAD OF THEM WAS a landscape unlike anything they could ever have dreamed of. At first Polly
and Lisa could only stand blinking in disbelief. It was
as if all the old pictures they had ever seen of ancient
civilisations had been rolled into one, but built on a
breathtaking scale. Multi-storeyed buildings, the size of
the tallest skyscrapers, stretched upwards. The tops of
the buildings seemed to be swathed in cloud-like mist.
These buildings had been built in a classical style, like
those in Rome or Florence, with arched windows and
buttresses and columns and statues, all beautifully
adorned with elaborate carvings.

Between the buildings, crisscrossing on more levels
than the girls could count, were what appeared at first
glance to be narrow glass highways, weaving in and out
of each other, round and sometimes straight through

the buildings themselves. But they weren't at all like roads at home.

'Wow, Polly,' exclaimed Lisa. 'Either I'm losing it, or they aren't roads at all. They're full of water! They're like canals – hundreds of canals.'

'They all seem to be going in different directions – and so fast,' said Polly.

On these canals were craft of various shapes and sizes, travelling with the flow of the water. Some even appeared to defy gravity and go uphill.

Polly spoke again. 'Can you make out what's running along beside them? There seem to be narrower paths a bit like pavements at the sides of roads – except they're not pavements at all. They're like swimming paths! Can you see? There are people in them being carried by the current.'

At certain points, rather like crossroads, it seemed that people could leave either the boats or the swimming paths they were travelling along to join others, presumably to refine their journey – a little like changing lines on a subway.

There were thousands of lights on every level, producing a strange, eerie glow that gave the whole place a not unpleasant greenish tinge. Every few minutes, the lights would flicker as if the power flow had been interrupted, making the whole place appear to shimmer and wobble.

Below them the ground vibrated ever so slightly, accompanied by a faint rumble, like a mighty engine throbbing way down in the bowels of the earth. The only other noise was the rushing of water.

'This has to be the all-time weirdest place in the world,' murmured Lisa.

'If we *are* still in the world,' said Polly grimly, staring at the inside of the glass wall which stretched far, far above. 'I keep feeling like I'm in a dream. Lisa, are you thinking what I'm thinking? This can't be where we come from, can it?' She trembled slightly at the idea, remembering the fish emblem on the front of the fishing boat.

'Well, we'll just have to find out. One thing's for sure though: this place is beautiful all right, but it's unreal – there's something dead creepy about it.'

'What do you reckon they're going to do with us?' asked Polly nervously.

'Well, I don't think they're going to *eat* us, despite the way we were caught. Hopefully they're going to talk to us and find out where we are from and then help us return. Hang on, aren't the guys asking us to follow them?'

The fishermen politely invited them to walk off the conveyor belt and up a narrow slipway to the nearest canal where an ornate little wooden boat was tied to the quay. It had padded seats with little handles at the sides to hang on to and the back looked like an elaborately carved fish tail. The rope was unhooked and the boat caught the current and began rushing along a waterway. They peered nervously around them, looking at the other canals above and below. As they were travelling, they watched as a small group of children dived into the narrow channel that ran beside them. These youngsters made little attempt to swim, but let the current carry them wherever it was going. They appeared to be wearing skin-tight suits, just like the fishermen.

'It's like a massive theme park,' cried Lisa, above the sound of the rushing water. 'It makes ours seem a bit wimpy.'

'Hang on, we're heading straight for that marble building,' said Polly.

Before they could work out what was happening, the little boat went through an archway, covered in carvings of animals and plants, and was steered into a tiny inlet that ran underneath the building. They headed towards a little speck of light in the distance and a few minutes later pulled up by some brightly lit steps, where the girls were asked to follow their hosts.

The outside of the building was magnificent enough, but the inside was more spectacular than the most sumptuous palace they had ever imagined. It was a mass of crystal and glistening white marble, with fountains and chandeliers and a million twinkling lights. Beautiful statues of what looked like gods, bedecked with carved flowers, adorned the walls, and weird music could be heard above the tinkling sound of the fountains.

Then they were led up a flight of stairs. At the top, a young man in a long, flowing toga was waiting for them. He, too, was tall and blond, with piercing green eyes. Although handsome, there was something about his movements that was strange, almost robotic. When he smiled, only his mouth moved. He asked them very politely to wait, then came back seconds later with two robes and ushered them to a small room where they were able to change out of their damp costumes. When they returned, he invited them to follow.

'I've never seen anything like this,' whispered Lisa. 'Who d'you reckon lives here? The king? Is *this guy* the king?'

Polly shrugged, unable to speak for fear that her voice would shake with nerves. They eventually came to a pair of lofty doors which seemed to be inlaid with mother of pearl and silver. There were two armed guards in strange uniforms on either side. Their young escort slipped inside and then returned seconds later.

'The master will see you now,' he declared with a deep bow, stepping aside to usher them in.

Chapter 7

POLLY AND LISA EDGED timidly into a magnificent room where an old man was seated on an ornate white sofa. As he rose to his feet, it was obvious how tall and imposing he must have been when younger. His deep-set eyes were the brightest green and they seemed to glow with a strange luminosity from under his heavy eyebrows. His long silver hair rested on the collar of a white tunic edged in silver. He strolled towards them with the aid of a silver cane which had a carved serpent wrapped around it. About his neck, on a thick chain, there hung a familiar jade fish – the same fish that the girls had on their backs. Was this the symbol of Fortuna?

Inclining his head towards them, he spoke in a deep, melodious voice. 'Welcome to Fortuna, my children. My name is Solon. I am the Imperial Governor. You must be very tired and not a little confused after your arduous journey. Would you like to sit down and take some refreshment with me?'

The girls looked at each other then at him. Not even Lisa trusted herself to speak in such an awe-inspiring environment.

'Please, don't be afraid,' he said. 'Nothing bad will happen to you here. Fortuna is a gentle place, full of light and good nature. I do hope you will enjoy living here.'

Polly and Lisa glanced at each other and frowned. Neither of them liked the sound of the word 'living', rather than 'visiting'.

A beautiful girl in a shimmering toga seemed to appear from nowhere and stood at Solon's side. He murmured something quietly to her and she bowed and disappeared as silently as she had arrived.

Lisa spoke first.

'What is this place?' she asked hesitantly.

'Do you really have no idea?' asked Solon, seemingly surprised.

She spoke with more assurance now. 'We were out swimming and we got sucked into a cave. Then these men came along in a big metal fish and brought us here. That's all we know.'

'Ah yes, I believe they were as surprised as you were. They only expected to catch fish, of course. They reported that you were lost in the middle of the ocean.'

'We still don't know where we are!' exclaimed Lisa. 'Could you tell us please?'

Before the governor could answer, the girl returned with a tray on which were two tall glasses and a large plate of what looked like small, fancy cakes. At once, the girls realised they hadn't eaten or drunk since breakfast. Without a second thought, they tucked in. The drinks were just about the most delicious and unusual they had ever tasted, but they swallowed the cakes so fast that they hardly had time to work out whether they tasted good or not.

'I think,' Solon said gently, when they had finished eating, 'that if you will bear with me, I should tell you a little of how Fortuna came to be. Please sit down and make yourselves comfortable – this could take a little time.

'It all came about,' he began, 'many, many years ago. There was a mighty volcanic eruption followed by an earthquake – by far the greatest the world had ever witnessed. The very plates forming the crust of the earth began to slip and slide and then sink beneath the oceans.

'At that time, the finest civilisation ever known was centred right at the point where the land began to sink. This civilisation contained many fine cities with beautiful buildings and these cities' scientific achievement and culture were more advanced than anything that had ever been seen before.

44

'After the violence of the initial earthquake, the descent into the water began very slowly. Every year the people noticed the ocean that surrounded them was creeping further inland . . .'

Lisa couldn't help thinking of all the recent threats of global warming back on the surface and what the experts said it was doing to sea levels. She began to say something about it to Polly, but Solon lifted his hand as if to silence her. He obviously wasn't used to being interrupted.

'All the little villages along the coast began to disappear,' he continued, 'and the people, mostly fishermen, who lived there, gradually moved up to higher ground. Then another, far more powerful earthquake struck and the water began to rise much faster. There was an emergency conference of the greatest minds in the land, who decided that as they couldn't make the waters go back, they must protect their beautiful cities – the cities which were their heritage. Many plans were put forward, but eventually they decided to put all their efforts and finances into building huge domes to cover seven of the greatest cities, and also to invent systems by which their populations could survive underwater. Every industry and every worker was employed in the making of glass bricks until thousands upon thousands were piling up all around our cities. As the waters rose, so did the glass walls. It was a race against time, with most of the cities, the ones unfortunate enough to be on lower ground, losing the race and being swallowed up before they could protect themselves. Millions of our people perished. Fortuna, having joined up with two other cities, finished the roof of its dome literally weeks before the waters engulfed it. It was all that remained of a mighty empire!

'How did the people breathe?' asked Polly.

'A very intelligent question, my dear,' replied Solon. 'Our great scientists of the time had worked together and developed a machine, the like and size of which had never been seen before, to break down water into its component parts and give the citizens the essential oxygen that they needed. The latest version is buried deep under the ground here and runs on geothermic power. The one we have now produces almost perfect air, as you can probably tell from the quality of the atmosphere.'

Polly and Lisa had to agree that apart from the occasional whiff of seaweed, the air around them was as clean and as fresh as back home.

Lisa whispered to Polly, 'So it's the air machine that makes the ground vibrate!'

Polly nodded, fascinated by Solon's story.

Lisa looked confused suddenly and addressed Solon. 'But couldn't the people all breathe underwater, like we can? If so, what was the big deal? Why did they need air? Why do you *still* need air?'

'More intelligent questions, my dear,' replied Solon with a smile. 'But let me continue, and I promise I'll explain later. Where was I? Oh, yes. The water continued to rise until the people were sadly forced to assume that the rest of the world must have been engulfed. Expeditions were sent up time and time again to try to reach the surface, but they came back saying that now we were miles underwater and that a vast impenetrable rock ceiling had slid over the cities.

'And the underwater breathing?' persisted Lisa.

Solon smiled again. 'Although the pressure is far too great to do so down here, we realised that it would be possible to swim in the sea above, where you were found. The great men of science decided to devote their time trying to find out how we could do that. They studied how fish managed to extract oxygen from the water and worked out that with fairly minor surgery, humans could do the same. What was truly amazing was that after many generations, babies began to be born not needing the operation. It was a kind of evolution, if you like.'

'And you've all lived down here ever since.'

'For better or worse, my ancestors were the last people alive, trapped in their crystal city at the bottom of an underground ocean.'

'But they weren't,' said Polly, rather bravely.

'I beg your pardon?' said Solon.

'They weren't the last people alive. We come from a world above the surface. There are millions of us up there.'

Solon's kindly look turned into a stare which became colder and colder. He then broke into a dry, cackling laugh.

'Nonsense, my dear. We know no such place exists. Although I have no idea where you come from, I don't believe that is a possibility.'

'But we *do* come from up there,' persisted Lisa, angrily. 'We have cars and planes and televisions and everything. And we have a huge sky with clouds and a big sun, and we want to go back there – now. We have people waiting for us.'

The governor was ignoring her now, and the patronising smile returned to his face. 'You are obviously very tired, my children. Being in the water for a long time can do very funny things to the mind if you're not used to it. Might I suggest you rest and then perhaps we may talk another time. I'm afraid I have many things to attend to. You will be shown to your quarters. I hope you will be very comfortable.'

'But you can't just keep us here,' said Polly, close to tears. 'We have parents and friends and things. They'll be worried sick.'

'When can we go home?' shouted Lisa, who was more cross than upset. 'It's against the law to hold people against their will, you know.' Even as she said it, she realised that no law from the world above could possibly count in Fortuna. It mattered little anyway – Solon was no longer listening to them. He had already turned on his heels and reached the door at the far end of his huge apartment.

Chapter 8

BACK ON THE SURFACE, the lifeboat and later a naval helicopter circled around Matt's boat. They continued searching for any signs of the missing girls until it was too dark to continue. Poor Matt hardly knew what was going on. He was used to things going exactly his way, and now he found himself in real trouble. The rescue teams had told him of the perils of diving in that area. Over the years, several divers had been reported missing and had never been found. It was believed that there was some underwater whirlpool, but nobody had ever lived to talk about it.

Matt explained over and over again what he and his two new friends had been doing, but the minute he mentioned that they had told him they could breathe underwater and that they'd dived over the side of the boat to prove it, any credibility he had was lost, and everyone he spoke to became suspicious. When Matt got back to the shore he was taken straight away to the local police station, where a rather stern looking detective sergeant took him into the interview room. He switched on a recorder and registered the date and the time.

'Now, young man, I think it's about time we had a bit of truth. You say you only met these two young women at the surf championships last Saturday.'

'Yeah, they came up to me after I'd got my trophy. I'd never seen them before. I just thought they were fans like the rest.'

'I see. And what did they say to you?'

'They just said the usual stuff about how they liked what I did – you know.'

The detective didn't know, but carried on. 'Why did you make a date with them for today? Did you fancy them or something?'

'No way! They were too young for me.'

'Oh, I see. But you still asked two complete strangers to come out for a ride in your father's boat?'

'So what? There's no harm in that, is there?' replied Matt beginning to feel a little annoyed. He'd never had anything to do with the police before and didn't like this man's presumption that he must have done something wrong.

'You told the coastguards that these girls said they

could breathe underwater. Didn't that strike you as a bit odd?'

'Yeah, course. But they seemed pretty normal in every other way. That was really the reason we went out in the first place. They were going to show me.'

Matt had considered mentioning the identical birthmarks, but realised that the detective would not take that seriously either, so didn't bother.

'So, let's get this right. Two complete strangers come up to you and tell you some cock and bull story about being able to do something that nobody has ever been able to do in the history of mankind and you believed them.'

'There has to be a first time,' said Matt with a little smile, despite the seriousness of the situation.

The policeman's sarcastic smile disappeared.

'Look, don't get funny with me, sonny. You are in serious trouble. Two young girls are missing, believed drowned, while out with you.'

'Listen,' said Matt, feeling his composure going, 'I've told you all I know. How do you think *I* feel? They were nice girls – I liked them. They just dived under the water and disappeared. I was sure they'd come up, but they didn't. I'm really gutted, just like everyone else. If it's my fault at all, it's for taking them out into such deep water – but that's it.'

'And you didn't even know their names?'

'Just their first names, like I told you – Polly and Lisa.'

'And they were only about thirteen or fourteen, you reckon.'

'As far as I know. I didn't ask. They looked about that, but you can't always tell, can you?'

'We've got some photos that were taken by the press when you were getting your prize. Perhaps you might be able to identify them.'

Most of the photos were of the three winners surrounded by a gaggle of fans, but a couple were taken just after, and one showed two girls talking to Matt.

'That's them, there,' said Matt nearly bursting into tears at seeing them again. 'That one's Polly and that's Lisa.'

The policeman relaxed, smiled and patted Matt on the shoulder.

'I might be going soft in my old age, son, but I'm beginning to believe you. It's not that I for one moment believe those girls really could or even thought they could breathe underwater, but perhaps that's what they told you. You've had a pretty rough day, so I think you'd better go home now. Don't go too far away, we'll need to talk to you again soon. I'll give this picture to the telly boys. We might be able to get it on the evening news. Someone must be missing them by now.'

Someone was. Lisa's gran had been concerned that

the two friends hadn't come back by six as expected. After a few hours, she'd rung the police, who told her the grim news.

The following morning, the search resumed in earnest. Local beaches were scoured and naval divers were called in, but when they were told the exact location of the dive, they were extremely cautious, and for safety reasons would not dive at depth. The police borrowed the latest submersible camera, but despite trailing it up and down deep underwater, it came up with nothing out of the ordinary. That night, the police and the coastguards called off the search with a statement that Polly and Lisa were missing, presumed dead.

Chapter 9

THE YOUNG MAN WHO had escorted Polly and Lisa to the governor now returned and beckoned to Polly and Lisa to follow. They were led through sumptuous corridors that were so wide they were almost like streets in their own right, lined with imposing statues and decorations.

Polly turned to Lisa. 'I can't work out whether we're inside or outside, seeing as outside's inside too.'

'I suppose it's better than being trapped in the water for ever.'

'We don't know what they're planning to do with us yet. I wonder what they're all thinking at home.' Polly fought to hold back the tears, as she imagined how worried her mother and father must be.

They turned a corner and approached what looked like an empty glass tank, suspended in crystal clear water. The young man ushered them in and when they looked around them, in amazement and fascination they saw they were actually in a tank within a tank, surrounded by thousands of the most brilliant multi-coloured tropical fish that swam right up to the glass and seemed every bit as interested in them.

'This must be what goldfish feel like,' murmured Lisa.

'Yeah, and *we* can't escape, either,' replied Polly gloomily.

When the young man pulled a small lever beside the door, a stream of bubbles from the roof caused the whole tank to descend slowly past several floors. When it came to a halt, the door opened, and the two girls followed him out into a bustling thoroughfare that reminded them of the lobbies of smart hotels on television. There were boutiques with expensive-looking clothing and jewellery and cafés with wealthy-looking people eating or simply relaxing over drinks.

Some of them were walking barefoot in the carpeted streets, and were wearing versions of the simple all-in-one suits that the fishermen had worn.

'I reckon they wear those so that they can swim whenever they want,' said Polly.

Lisa nodded. 'Have you noticed? Most of them have fairly short hair. It must be so that it dries off quickly.'

'And they all have the same colouring. *Our* colouring!

There are no black people or people of any other colours come to that.'

'And everyone seems pretty fit and young and good-looking,' whispered Lisa.

They eventually came to a little passageway that led to a series of ornate doors. One of them, up a short flight of stairs, opened into a large, stylish apartment.

'This is where you will stay,' said the young man, in his slightly robotic voice. 'I think you should find everything you need, but if there is anything else, just pull on the bell. I will be only too happy to serve you. My name is Petruvio, by the way.' With that, he bowed deeply and, before they could say a word, smiled his cold smile again, and closed the door quietly behind him.

'Oh my God!' squeaked Lisa at once. 'What have we gone and got ourselves into now? Is this cosmic or what?'

'I can't believe I'm not dreaming,' said Polly. 'Like, what's going on? This is the sort of place film stars live. I've seen worse in *Hello!* magazine.'

The apartment was huge. A map of Fortuna hung in the spacious hall, and several rooms opened off it. There was a luxurious sitting room with a large pool in the middle. The pool was surrounded by numerous enticing bottles and bowls, which contained exotic soaps and essences. At one end of it was a pile of snowy white towels, at the other was a fountain firing tiny rainbow-coloured crystal droplets towards the high ceiling. In mirrored wardrobes in the two bedrooms they found lots of clothes on hangers and racks. Most of them were like loose tracksuits in fine materials, but there were several of the tight, figure-hugging suits they had seen people wearing outside; presumably they were everyday wear for travelling on the canals. Lisa pulled out a few and both agreed they were beautiful and surprisingly stylish.

'Shall we share?' said Polly, bouncing on an enormous bed. 'This bed's big enough for six of us.'

'You're not kidding. You'd never catch me sleeping alone in this place – especially with Petruvio hanging around. He might be fit, but he's really creepy.'

'Do you remember *Thunderbirds*? They were these puppets who were supposed to be rescue agents. I think he looks a bit like one of them.'

'I know what you mean,' said Polly sadly. At this reminder of happily watching TV at home, her mood suddenly changed. 'I'm sorry, Lisa, I keep thinking about my poor mum and dad. They must think we've drowned. And what about Matt? He's probably in real trouble.'

'You know when that Solon guy said he hoped we'd enjoy *living* here?' asked Lisa. 'It gave me the creeps. Surely they won't force us to stay here, will they?'

'I think we should ask to see him again. Then we'll make sure he tells us when we can go home.'

Polly lay back on the bed. 'I've been thinking about our meeting with Solon . . . You know when we told him about the surface and everything and he said he didn't believe us? I think he was lying. The way his face changed when we talked about it – he looked really shocked for a moment. I reckon he knows only too well there's a world up there. Where else could we have come from?'

Lisa looked puzzled. 'I know what you're saying, but then why wouldn't he want to know more about it, eh?'

'Don't know,' replied Polly. 'Maybe he doesn't want to. Maybe he knows it already. I'm beginning to think this might be like a posh prison. Do you think we can even leave this apartment?'

'We haven't tried to go out yet.'

Their eyes met and without saying another word, the two girls leaped off the bed and dashed down the corridor to the front door. It was locked.

'How dare they! We're shut in. Let's ring the bell and get what's his name back. Maybe he'll listen to us.'

Polly pulled the bell chord and a couple of minutes later the door opened and Petruvio came in, still with a creepy smile on his face.

'Is there anything I can get you?' he asked politely.

'Yeah, you can get us out of here. Plus, we want to talk to you,' Lisa said firmly.

Petruvio looked a little awkward, and seemed to

struggle to maintain his smile. 'I'm afraid I can't help you.'

'We want to tell you about our world above,' said Polly quietly.

Petruvio looked flustered, and the smile disappeared. 'I'm sorry,' he replied, 'but if that is all, I must leave.'

'Who told you not to speak to us?' Lisa shouted, beginning to lose her temper. 'Was it Solon?'

'I c-can't . . .' he stuttered, terribly anxious now. 'Please ring if there is anything you require.' With that he slipped out of the door and closed it behind him. The girls dashed to open it but it was locked again.

'Do you think this place is bugged?' asked Polly, trying not to panic.

'We don't know what's been invented down here yet. Let's hope not.'

'We definitely need to see the governor again. We're obviously not going to get anything out of Petruvio,' said Lisa.

She pulled on the bell once more and minutes later Petruvio came through the door again.

He bowed deeply. 'Is there anything I can do for you?'

'Yes,' said Lisa crossly. 'We want to see the governor – Solon.'

The young man looked confused now. 'I'm sorry, but

the master is a very busy man. I don't know if that will be possible.'

It was Polly's turn to speak. As always, she was slightly calmer and politer than her friend. 'Look, we really need to see him . . . *Pleeeease!* There are people missing us at home. We need to get back. They'll be worried.' She was on the verge of tears.

Petruvio's robotic face softened and his expression seemed almost sympathetic for a moment. 'I will see what I can do.'

Chapter 10

AFTER PETRUVIO HAD LEFT, Polly and Lisa found a door that they hadn't noticed before. It led into a small room which was like a huge store cupboard with numerous different compartments and what looked like a dining table, laid for two people. The compartments were full of all sorts of weird and wonderful foods and drinks. Despite the snack in Solon's office, neither of them had realised how hungry they were now until they started eating. There were little pies that tasted rather like chicken and ham and some delicious crunchy greens that reminded Lisa of the spicy seaweed she'd once tried in a Chinese restaurant. Polly's favourite was a dish similar to spaghetti, but with a tangy sauce she didn't recognise. They both chose a drink that tasted like the smoothies they had at home.

'This is all very weird,' said Polly, in between mouth-fuls. 'It's almost as if they were expecting us.'

Just as they'd finished eating Petruvio returned. 'The master says he will see you in the morning,' he said. 'I will return to take you there.'

'Does that mean we're stuck in here until then?'

'I will come back for you in the morning,' he repeated, and hurried away before they could question him further.

Just then, a loud siren filled the air. The girls slid the curtains in the bedroom to one side, just in time to watch the lights dim all over the city. The canals began to empty of craft and swimmers. In ten minutes the waterways were completely deserted, apart from a few sinister-looking boats with searchlights, carrying men dressed like the guards who had stood outside Solon's door. Then it went completely dark.

'Do you know what? I reckon no one's allowed out at night. I bet those official-looking blokes are checking that everyone's gone home,' said Lisa.

'Are you still scared?' asked Polly when they were in bed, but she almost knew what Lisa's answer would be.

Lisa was silent for a second. 'A bit. Well, I was. Funny, isn't it? Of course I ought to be. I don't know why, but I don't think they're going to hurt us. Solon seems all right to me. I'm more worried about what everyone back home is thinking. It's awful that they might think we're dead.'

Polly knew Lisa was probably braver than she was, but she didn't exactly feel threatened here either. She thought about her mother and father at home. She had never ever given them reason to worry before. Well, she'd certainly made up for that now. She lay on her side of the bed, staring at the ceiling and wondering what was to become of them, but owing to their eventful and exhausting day she soon fell fast asleep.

In the morning, a voice woke them abruptly. It was Petruvio – and he was at the bedroom door.

'Good morning,' he said, smiling pleasantly. 'I do hope you slept well. If you would like to get yourselves ready and have your breakfast, I will come back for you in a little while.'

'Where are we going?' asked Lisa sleepily, blinking at nothing in particular, and not really expecting an answer.

'The master will see you a little later,' he announced curtly. 'I will escort you there.'

When they had bathed in the pool, which had miraculously become hot and steamy overnight, they dressed in their new clothes. They both chose the all-in-one skin-tight outfits that they had seen people swimming in. Polly's was the most brilliant metallic blue and Lisa's a deep sea-green. In spite of themselves, they couldn't help but feel rather excited. Petruvio escorted them back to see Solon. He was seated, as before, in his palatial office.

'Ah, there you are, young ladies,' he said in his deep but friendly voice. 'How nice to see you again. I do hope you have been looked after well. I believe you have some questions for me.'

'We would like to know how long we are going to have to stay here,' Lisa came out with straightaway. 'And why we are being kept prisoner?'

Solon smiled. 'You are not prisoners, my dear. Petruvio will take you wherever you want to go. Last night the doors were locked because it was nearly dark-time. We didn't want anything to happen to you, did we? It will be fine when you know your way around. As for how long you will stay, I'm afraid there really are very few alternatives. You say you come from a land above the water, but even if there was one, we know of no way of getting you back there. Why are you so anxious to leave?'

'Because we are away from our parents and all our friends,' said Polly frantically. 'We've nothing against Fortuna, but surely you won't keep us here if we don't want to stay?'

'I'm sure when you realise how wonderful life is here,

you will forget about everything else. Everyone is extremely happy here.'

'Why won't Petruvio talk to us?' Lisa asked. 'As soon as we ask any questions he runs away.'

Solon rubbed his chin. 'As I said, everyone is quite content with their lives here in Fortuna. They do not want to hear of other, imaginary worlds. Do you understand?'

As he spoke, his expression hardened. He threw them a piercing glance that almost made their blood freeze.

'Now,' he said, returning to his usual, friendly tone, 'is there anything else you'd like to ask?'

'Where does everyone go when you turn the lights down?' asked Lisa.

'Aaah, that is the time when the citizens of Fortuna return to their homes. It is for their own protection. There are some evil people around who are extremely dangerous. They come out at dark-time.'

'What do they want?' asked Polly.

'They are devoted to overthrowing the tranquillity of Fortuna.'

'Where do they come from?'

'It is difficult to say exactly. There is an area called the Southern Quarter which is a labyrinth of desolate and decrepit buildings. We think they could be based there. But they are like vermin – we can seldom find them.

When we do, however, we punish them severely.' As he said this, his mouth twisted into a sadistic smile.

'Are we going to be allowed to meet people of our own age?' enquired Lisa, changing the subject again.

'Of course,' the old man said, beaming. 'Who would you like to meet?'

Lisa looked puzzled. 'Well, we don't know yet. How could we?'

'Of course you don't. How silly of me.' Solon walked over to a window that looked out on to a kingdom that was now covered in lights. 'I'm sure when you settle down, you will have lots of friends. Now, once more, I hope you will excuse me, but being Governor keeps me very busy.'

'But we need to get home,' said Lisa, trying hard to contain her anger. 'Can you help us?'

The governor walked back to his desk, rang a bell and Petruvio returned immediately.

'We thought you might like to have a proper tour of Fortuna,' said Solon. 'Perhaps you would like to go with Petruvio.'

Despite their earlier doubts about Petruvio, both Polly and Lisa agreed later that day that he was one of the most handsome young men they had come across, even in a place like Fortuna where *everybody* seemed to be good-looking. His blond hair was slightly wavy, and his teeth were the whitest they had ever seen. Polly had commented that had he been up on earth he could well have been a model or a pop star. He had the perfect swimmer's body – like many of the young men they had seen already – but he was slightly more muscular than the others. His main problem, however, was that he seemed continually ill at ease and had no sense of humour whatsoever.

Petruvio escorted the girls to a small boat which was moored a short distance from the governor's office. He untied the rope and soon the little craft was gliding along a lofty canal at a fair pace. After about fifteen minutes he steered it to the side and escorted Polly and Lisa down a small staircase where another boat was waiting on a narrower canal, that went off at a right angle. This time they flew down a waterfall at breakneck speed, whizzing over and under a series of larger canals that crisscrossed the city. It was just about the most exciting ride the girls had ever taken and for a while they shrieked and laughed, almost forgetting their circumstances. The swimmers in the slipway to the side took the experience for granted and chatted nonchalantly amongst themselves as they sped along.

After another half an hour, the girls noticed that they were leaving the beautiful city and travelling through an area where there were hundreds of small fields of what looked like fruit trees and other crops – all at various stages of maturity. From what they could gather from Petruvio, Fortuna consisted of one huge city (also called Fortuna) surrounded by fields. He made no mention of any other towns.

'Don't you think it all looks a little too good to be true?' Lisa asked Polly quietly, while Petruvio wasn't paying attention.

'I know what you mean,' whispered Polly. 'I haven't seen one person, man or woman, doing any actual work. These crops can't look after themselves or pick themselves come to that, can they? Somebody must have to do it. There don't even seem to be any cottages for workers to live in.'

'Everything grows well here,' said Petruvio, rejoining the conversation. 'It is because we can control the climate to suit our needs. Thanks to our scientific discoveries we can grow corn and many other crops in a matter of weeks.'

'Sounds like a form of genetic engineering, if you ask me,' Polly whispered to Lisa.

'Do you have animals like cows and pigs and chickens and stuff?' she asked Petruvio, remembering the food they'd eaten the night before.

'I have read in some of our ancient books of such things, but we have none of them – we only use the creatures from the water around us.'

'Doesn't that get a bit boring?' asked Lisa, who had never been very fond of seafood.

'I think you will agree that we have something to suit everyone's taste.'

The girls had to agree that what they'd been offered so far had been extremely good, but it still seemed like all Petruvio's answers had been programmed.

'So what do you do for fun?' asked Lisa, cheekily.

Petruvio looked puzzled. 'I'm sorry, could you explain?'

'What would young people like us do to enjoy themselves?'

'What everyone else does – read our ancient books, watch plays and discuss the classics. Then, of course, there is swimming. Practically everything we do involves the water. We are about to have our annual championships.'

Polly and Lisa suddenly sprang to attention.

'What championships?' asked Polly.

'They're called the Aquagames and it is where we decide who are the greatest swimmers in our country. Do you like swimming?'

'We love it!' exclaimed Lisa. 'It's what we do best.'

'Then you must come,' said Petruvio, pleased to have found some common ground at last. 'It will be a way for you to meet people. You will need friends if you are to live amongst us.'

Lisa suddenly snapped. 'Look, we told you, and we told Solon: we don't want to stay. We have no intention of living here. Doesn't anyone listen to a word we say?'

The two girls found the rest of the tour fascinating, despite their worries at being kept against their will. By changing canals a few times they were able to see many different places. At one point they came to an area with large, tall factories where, Petruvio explained, all the things that were necessary in everyday life – from furniture to machinery – were manufactured. The buildings were still beautiful, but less ornamental than those in the city. Most striking of all were the huge chimneys that stretched right up as far as the eye could see.

'The chimneys take all the steam out of our dome,' continued Petruvio, rather like a tour guide. 'Did you notice the streams of bubbles as you were arriving?'

'How do you keep your houses warm?' asked Polly.

'We don't need to. We keep the atmosphere throughout the dome at a constant temperature. It took centuries to get it right. All the energy we need is tapped from way down close to the earth's core.'

'So there are no summers or winters?'

Petruvio looked puzzled for a moment, but then brightened as if he had just remembered. 'Our history books tell us about these seasons in the days before the great flood.'

'We have them where we come from,' said Lisa nostalgically, realising that they had been told by Solon not to mention such things. She continued nonetheless. 'And an autumn and spring too.'

Petruvio stared at her for a split-second. She could have sworn he was dying to know more. It was then that a look of pure fear crossed his handsome face.

'You must not talk of such things. I have been ordered not to listen.'

Polly felt almost sorry for him. 'What will happen if you do? We won't tell – promise.'

He had gone slightly pale. 'P-please don't ask any more. Awful things can happen here if you disobey. I must leave it at that. I've already said far too much. It isn't that I don't want to know anything, but it is easier if I don't. Can you understand?'

Polly and Lisa exchanged a worried glance. It was obvious that poor Petruvio had been put in an awful position and that it was more than his life was worth to have a free and open conversation with them. There was something very, very wrong with Fortuna, but they weren't sure what it was. Everyone they'd seen so far looked so content, but the girls were beginning to wonder if they were hiding something. When Polly and Lisa returned to their room that evening, they certainly had lots of things to discuss.

Chapter 11

BACK IN ENGLAND, LIFE was slowly beginning to settle down. The girls' parents and friends were devastated by their loss, but in many ways it was Matt who was suffering most, because he couldn't help feeling that the accident was his fault. The memorial service was supposed to be a small and intimate affair but, predictably, the press had whipped it up into a huge media extravaganza, with television cameras and reporters fighting each other for stories. Matt had met both Polly's and Lisa's adoptive parents and his honest approach and obvious sorrow had convinced them that he was not responsible for their disappearance. He didn't mention the strange mark they shared, for fear of complicating everything even more.

A warning was put out about the area of sea where the girls had disappeared and naturally the mutterings amongst the locals reached fever pitch. There were now rumours of sea monsters of a size and ferocity never heard of before, and it wasn't long before some of the old-timers began claiming that they had seen them. Local fishermen, famous for their superstitions, now sailed miles out of their way to avoid losing their precious boats.

The police had more or less given up as far as Matt was concerned. There was no evidence of any violence on the boat, which might have suggested foul play. Both girls had been good swimmers, and – apart from the bizarre claim that they had said they could breathe underwater – there was nothing to disprove Matt's version of events.

Matt himself was very confused. At the first opportunity he had tried breathing underwater himself, but he'd given up almost immediately when he'd nearly drowned; as far as he was concerned, it was impossible. He spent a lot of time alone, driving his motorbike along the coastline, looking in every creek and cave he could find, hoping against hope that he *wouldn't* find their drowned bodies. He just couldn't accept that the girls would leave the boat so confidently and stay underwater so long, if they couldn't breathe underwater. He knew he could never rest until he had solved the mystery of their disappearance.

* * *

The World Surfing Championships, held in Australia, were coming up in a week's time. Just as Matt was about to book his flight, he received a strange phone call.

'Hello, is that Matt Miller? Look, you don't know me, but I managed to get your number from your fan club. I told them I was your long-lost cousin . . . sorry. It's dead important, honest. My name's Kelly Peters and it's to do with the two girls who went missing.'

Matt had had many nuisance phone calls before and since the accident, and he was used to dealing with them politely but firmly, but before he had a chance to say anything Kelly continued.

'My dad's in the RAF, see, and we've been in Germany since I was a kid. We've just come back to the UK because he's been posted to an airbase here. Well, I heard all about those poor girls and something really got to me. It was the bit where you said they'd told you they could breathe underwater. I know it sounds weird, but I'd always thought I might be able to.'

Matt suddenly felt really angry. 'Are you pulling my leg? If you are it's *so* not funny.'

'No, I'm not, I promise. Listen, I've always been really good at swimming and I'm in the local swimming club. Just recently I've been going to our local pool by myself and trying to do this breathing thing. I don't really know why but I felt almost like I had to. Anyway, it didn't work at first, but I tried again and again, and suddenly it was as if a little valve suddenly opened in my head.'

'What are you saying? You're not telling me you can breathe underwater, too?'

'Yes, I am. I can do it perfectly now.'

Matt's voice rose an octave. 'Have you told anyone?'

'No one at all, apart from you – not even my parents. It's funny, but for some reason I don't want to.'

Matt remembered Polly and Lisa saying exactly the same thing.

'Look,' he nearly shouted, 'I've got to meet you. This is so important.'

Kelly lived in Abingdon in Oxfordshire – not the most convenient place for Matt, but he had a motorbike. They arranged to meet in the café at Kelly's swimming pool the next day.

When Matt walked into the café he knew who Kelly was instantly. He was struck by how like the other girls she was in build and stature – tall, broad-shouldered and loose-limbed. She too had bright green wide-set eyes and blond hair.

They introduced themselves rather formally and without further ado, Kelly got changed and led Matt to the pool. Luckily, apart from a few kids in the shallow end, there was hardly anyone around.

Kelly dived into the deep water and promptly swam

three widths without surfacing. Matt was amazed when the bubbles stopped and he realised that she must, indeed, be breathing underwater. When she finally came out of the pool, he was speechless. This had put a whole new light on the disappearance of Polly and Lisa and he felt suddenly alive and excited for the first time in ages.

They walked outside in a heavy silence and sat on a bench in the sunshine. Matt knew he had to tell Kelly the full story of how Polly and Lisa had disappeared.

He told her all about his first meeting with the girls. When he got to the part when they mentioned the birthmark, Kelly interrupted him.

'Sorry, what sort of mark?'

'Hang on a minute, I'll show you,' said Matt. He lifted the back of his shirt and she had a really close look at it.

'I don't have anything like that,' said Kelly, almost sadly. 'Mind you, I can't say I've spent a lot of time looking. Did you notice when I was in the pool?'

'No – I was too busy watching you breathe underwater. Shall I have a look?'

Matt realised it was a little odd, inspecting the back of a girl he'd only just met, but this was no ordinary situation. As Kelly lifted the back of her T-shirt he spotted the tiny mark immediately.

Kelly was shocked and also a little frightened when he told her she had it too.

Matt looked very serious. 'Kelly, I've got to ask you one more thing. Where were you were born?'

Kelly was surprised at the question. 'Why, what's that got to do with anything? If you must know, I was born in the local hospital just up the road.'

Matt seemed disappointed. He explained the other strange connection between him and the two girls – how they had been abandoned and adopted.

'Not me! My mum and dad would have told me. Well, if I'd just been found as a baby they wouldn't even be my mum and dad, would they?'

'Are you completely sure?' asked Matt, fully aware of what a shock it would be to find out something like that at her age.

'Of course I'm sure.'

Matt didn't press her. His mind was preoccupied. If Kelly and the two girls could swim underwater without breathing, he was now certain he could too.

'Look, do you think you could help me breathe underwater? I've got nowhere near – but I'm sure I must be able to.'

Matt had a pair of surf shorts in his backpack, and wanted to have a lesson there and then.

'Remember,' said Kelly, when Matt had got into the pool, 'when you're under the surface, try to blow out through your ears, as hard as you can. Try not to think about air.'

Matt did it a few times but came spluttering to the surface, gasping for breath. It was on the fifth attempt that something strange happened. Something seemed to give way in the front of his head, just behind his nose. He pulled in a huge breath of water and pushed it as hard as he could through his ears and mouth. Instead of needing the life-sustaining air he found he could survive by simply repeating the process. He even felt the water leaving through his ears. At last he had cracked it! He leaped out of the water and hugged Kelly, making her almost as wet as he was. He now knew for certain there was something very special about all of them – Polly, Lisa, this girl called Kelly and now him.

When Matt finally left, Kelly had a lot on her mind. There were so many coincidences – the only difference between her and the others was that she had not been abandoned as a baby. The more she thought about it, the more concerned she became about the truth of her situation. After all, she'd always thought that she didn't look anything like her parents.

Kelly was an impetuous girl. She decided to put any doubts to rest immediately. When she arrived home, she went straight to her mother and father. They were in the garden, having tea.

'Are you all right, darling?' asked her mother. 'You look like you've seen a ghost.'

'I was talking to someone today who said that I might be adopted,' Kelly said without even bothering to say hello.

Her parents stared at one another. There was complete silence as each hoped the other would say something. Her mother was the first to speak.

'Who told you that, darling?'

'Look, does it matter? Just tell me it isn't true.'

Her father looked fleetingly at her mother and then stood up and walked slowly round the garden table towards her.

'I don't know who could have told you, or why, but . . . I'm afraid it is true, darling. We never knew when the right time to tell you was. Maybe we should have said something when you were little. Your mother and I discussed it a lot, but then, as time went by, it didn't seem to matter. You were our beautiful daughter, we loved you more than anything.'

Kelly was distraught. 'You should have told me!' she cried out in tears, and raced to her room in a complete daze. She wanted to make some kind of sense of it all. So many things had happened in the last couple of weeks and now her mother and father, whom she loved so much, turned out not to be her real ones.

After a while there was a knock at her door. Her mother came in and sat next to her on the bed, and told her the whole story of her adoption – how she had been found on the beach in Cornwall, wrapped in seaweed. Her real parents were never traced. Kelly's mother explained how she and her father had been unable to have their own children and had fallen in love with Kelly on sight. Kelly felt awash with different emotions. She managed to give her mother a weak smile and said she just needed to be alone at the moment.

As she got over the initial shock of her parents not being her birth parents, she started to think about everything else. So where *had* she come from? Why could she breathe underwater? What did the little fish symbol mean? Who were these new people in her life – Matt and the two girls who'd disappeared? And who were her real parents? She felt very alone.

It was the middle of the night when she decided she had to call Matt. He too was unable to sleep and was wide awake when his mobile rang.

'It's true,' Kelly blurted out without even introducing herself. 'My parents adopted me and they don't know who my real ones are. I was abandoned like all of you. Hey look, what does it all mean? Please tell me!'

Matt's first reaction was to feel relieved. He had found the responsibility of all this almost too much to bear. Now at least he could share it with someone.

'I don't know, but I've been doing some serious thinking too,' he said quietly. 'Knowing for sure that it's possible to breathe underwater means that Polly and

Lisa may not have drowned after all. I'm pretty sure this is not over yet and I'm so pleased I can't tell you.'

'How do you mean?'

'Well, I think the girls might have swum somewhere else, or been kidnapped or something – I don't know. But I think they're still alive.'

'Kidnapped? Like where and who by?'

'Look, I just don't know. Maybe they just swam off somewhere for a laugh.'

'Not much of a laugh,' said Kelly, 'making people think you're dead. Were they the sort who'd have got a kick out of that?'

'No, I don't think so – they seemed really straight.'

'Anyway it was weeks ago,' said Kelly. 'Surely they'd have turned up by now, if it was a joke.'

'I think you're right. Look, Kelly, I hardly knew them, but even so I don't think they'd have pulled a stunt like that. I reckon something, or someone, is keeping them against their will.'

Chapter 12

THE NEXT FEW WEEKS passed quickly in Fortuna. Polly and Lisa were allowed to go out, but only if accompanied by Petruvio. At first they quite enjoyed it, as they travelled to and fro by canal and swimway. The all-in-one costumes that they had found in their wardrobes turned out to be made of something quite remarkable, for as soon as they left the water and shook themselves, they were dry. It was odd to walk around wearing so little, but always be warm. During the day they wore nothing else. Best of all Fortuna's delights were the water shoots that they discovered in the main squares. These spiralled down from the top level of the dome to the bottom in a near vertical, helter-skelter free fall. Coming down these was about the most exciting thing they had ever done.

Polly and Lisa's other favourite aspect of Fortunan

life was the free food and drink dispensers. At the end of every arcade there would be a long row of small windows, offering a selection of food and drink of every description. There were all manner of unusual salads and exotic fish dishes as well as delicious sweets and confectionary. All one had to do was lift the glass front and take what one wanted – and all for free. The girls were dying to find out how the people who ran Fortuna could possibly afford it. For a start, as far as they could make out, nobody really seemed to do any work. Petruvio had told them that money, as such, didn't exist and that everything worked on a merit system. If you did good deeds for the community, he said, you were awarded merits over and above the ones you were issued as a matter of course. These automatic merits seemed to allow the population a luxurious, carefree lifestyle.

The atmosphere in Fortuna was pleasant enough, but although everyone seemed to go about their business in a reasonably cheerful manner, the two friends couldn't help thinking that it was all rather superficial. There was nothing they could put their finger on, but every-thing just seemed too good to be true. People were polite and quite helpful, but nobody asked them a single question, which seemed very odd – two young people had suddenly appeared from nowhere, and no one wanted to know more about it. It was almost as if everyone had been ordered not to ask questions – but by whom and more to the point, why?

Added to this, wherever they went, both girls felt sure that they were being watched. Not necessarily in a sinister way, but watched all the same.

When the siren went off to herald the lights going off, they noticed that everybody stopped what they were doing immediately and headed for their homes as if afraid to do otherwise. Everybody seemed to be like Petruvio – little more than robots, programmed to do exactly as they were told. Underneath, Polly and Lisa sensed a deep fear – but of what, they could only guess.

Worst of all, no one ever really laughed. It was as if the capacity for seeing the funny side of things had been removed. The Fortunans would smile graciously and sometimes even say things that could, in other circumstances, be regarded as quite amusing – but laughter . . . never. A good example of this occurred when Petruvio slipped on the edge of a swimway and toppled into the water, soaking the people around him. Both Polly and Lisa howled with laughter, but Petruvio simply looked confused. He wasn't angry, but he just didn't seem to understand why they were laughing.

The two girls also realised that there were some areas of Fortuna that were only talked about in hushed voices and because Petruvio never took them there, they worked out that these areas must be out of bounds.

Every now and again they would just catch the words that Solon had mentioned weeks ago – the Southern Quarter. But when they tried to find out more about this place, they were once again met with a wall of silence. On the map of Fortuna that hung in their apartment, no reference to such a place was marked.

When Lisa asked Petruvio what happened if you broke laws in Fortuna, again she was met with silence. It was as if such things never occurred. Both girls were left with the distinct feeling that underlying all this apparent ease and prosperity was a dark secret. A secret which they became obsessed with finding out.

Despite their worries, the two friends spent a lot of time in the various pools, lakes and swimways. It felt good to be exercising again. They met many other young people who were, as they had expected, friendly and helpful but, as always, they never felt they could get to know them properly. Polly and Lisa found they had little in common with people who had lived all their lives in a glass bubble under the sea.

One day they were resting by a lake, having just swum for a couple of hours. There were a couple of girls sitting next to them. As usual, Petruvio was nearby, but he didn't seem to be listening. Polly and Lisa were both in a mischievous mood.

Polly began the conversation.

'Do you know Petruvio over there? He's our sort of guardian.'

The older of the two girls turned to look at him. 'We've seen him about. He lives in the Imperial Governor's palace.'

'Do you like him? We do.'

'What do you mean?'

'Do you fancy him? He's very good-looking, isn't he?'

The girl, who was rather beautiful herself, frowned. 'I'm sorry, I'm not sure what you mean.'

'Would you like to go out with him?'

'Out? Out where?'

'Well, you know, just go somewhere alone, just you and him.'

'Why?'

Lisa realised the two girls hadn't a clue what they were talking about and broke in. 'Don't you have anything like parties and cinemas and stuff like that, where young people go in the evening?'

The girl looked puzzled and ill at ease. 'We go home in the evenings, to our parents.'

It was Lisa's turn to look puzzled. 'How do you meet boys then, to . . . well, you know? Where we come from, boys and girls are always pairing off and . . .'

They sensed Petruvio standing over them. He had obviously been listening to the last part of their conversation.

'It is time to go,' he said in a cold, strict and slightly angry voice. 'We have things to do.'

The two Fortunan girls walked away, talking intensely to each other.

'No, we don't,' cried Lisa indignantly. 'Why do we have to leave? We were in the middle of talking to them, in case you hadn't noticed.'

'You were about to discuss where you come from. You know you cannot do that.'

'I just wanted to know how girls and boys get together in this place.'

Petruvio smiled slightly. 'In Fortuna, all liaisons are organised by the authorities. They spend a long time finding who is suitable for whom. It is the way we keep ourselves pure. When it is decided, the two young people are then told they can live together in an apartment that is supplied for them by the authorities. It is very simple.'

'Will that happen to you?'

'I will be paired in two years' time when I am twenty. The authorities have already begun to investigate candidates for my future partner.'

'But what if you don't fancy them?' asked Polly.

Petruvio looked confused. He obviously didn't know the word 'fancy' in this context.

'What if you don't feel as if you want to kiss her and stuff?' said Lisa, giggling behind her hand.

A look of fear came into Petruvio's eyes. 'We must go,' he said forcefully. 'It will be dark-time soon and we are a long way from home.'

Chapter 13

TIME PASSED. POLLY AND LISA learned that if you didn't ask awkward questions, life jogged along quite nicely in Fortuna. But there were some things they never got used to. They hated the dark-time curfew more than anything else and missed the freedom and unpredictability of life back home, like messing about with mates, having a laugh, breaking the rules now and again and staying out late – it was all unheard of in Fortuna as were so many of the things that were part of everyday life back on the surface. Most of all, during the long, boring evenings, they missed their parents and their friends. They talked endlessly about what might be happening back home. If only there was a way to contact their parents, or Matt, and let them know they were still alive. They were now beginning to hate Fortuna and everything it stood for.

'Do you have schools here like we have at home?' Lisa asked Petruvio one morning.

By now, Petruvio had become deeply suspicious of any conversations with the girls. He was never sure where their questions might be leading.

'We have schools where children go between the ages of four and sixteen. After that we go in small groups to be taught by our learned men.'

'Where did you go to school?'

'I am different. My family are part of the Imperial Household. We had private teachers who came to the governor's palace.'

Polly and Lisa glanced at each other. So that was why Petruvio seemed so aloof. He was obviously part of the ruling class.

'What do you study?'

'We study science and mathematics, music and art.'

'What about geography?' asked Lisa, with a wicked little smile. Polly realised what this was leading to and felt nervous.

'I'm sorry, I don't know what that is.'

'It is the study of all the different places in the world and how they have developed. Surely you must want to know what you are missing – all the wonderful countries and rivers and mountains and —'

Petruvio was suddenly furious. 'If you continue to

goad me in this way I shall speak with my uncle, the governor, and he will confine you to your quarters until your fate is decided.'

Ah, thought Lisa. So Petruvio is closely related to Solon.

That evening, Polly and Lisa were summoned to appear before Solon. This time he seemed cold and aloof and rather frightening. He spoke slowly and firmly.

'I hear you have continued to talk about the place you claim to have come from. I do not want you talking about it to Petruvio, or anyone else come to that.'

'We just thought he might be interested, that's all. And it feels natural for us to talk about our home,' said Lisa bravely. Polly nodded in solidarity.

The old man stood to his full height and glowered down through narrowed eyes at the two friends. 'I do not seem to be making myself clear. If you cannot desist from this behaviour, I will only have one alternative.'

Too terrified to ask, Polly and Lisa waited to hear what that alternative might be.

Although Solon spoke quietly, he sounded even more menacing. 'Let us say we have a place where people who find it difficult to abide by our rules go. Now is that completely clear? The choice is yours.'

Polly and Lisa nodded slowly and chose, once again, not to speak.

* * *

That night they lay in bed, discussing what Solon had said long into the night. They realised that Petruvio, the nephew of Solon, must be treated with the deepest suspicion. They were now sure that anything they asked or said would be instantly relayed back to the Imperial Governor.

From that point on, Polly and Lisa's conversations with Petruvio were limited only to subjects that were 'approved' by the authorites – like swimming, fashion, fine food and Fortuna's glorious architecture and history.

Despite this, the two friends learned a great range of facts from Petruvio. This society that had been cut off so dramatically in its prime, had developed along completely different lines from their world. Fortuna's brilliant scientists and engineers had improved and refined steam and waterpower, for instance, beyond anything known before. They had also developed clock-work to a fine art, with many machines that would have run on electricity on the surface having to be wound up.

'Do you realise we've been here over a month?' Polly said one morning as they were having breakfast.

Lisa sighed deeply. 'Is it only that long? It feels as if I've been here half my life. You know, if we don't do something soon, we'll be here for ever. Living here's driving me crazy. I reckon I'd do just about anything to escape now.'

Lisa and Polly had been having this same conversation on a daily basis. They also spent many hours discussing their origins. It seemed obvious from the Fortunans' looks and physique and from the fact that they could breathe underwater that the girls really did come from Fortuna. So somehow, for some reason, they must have been taken up to the surface as babies. That meant, surely, that some person or persons in Fortuna had taken them.

'There must be a way through that rock ceiling, otherwise we couldn't have got up there in the first place.'

'Brilliant!' exclaimed Lisa. 'So it's just a matter of finding a tiny hole in a vast rock ceiling outside that dome somewhere then. That should be nice and easy – I don't think.'

'Why do you think we were chosen to go to the surface as babies?' asked Polly, ignoring her friend's sarcasm. 'What was so special about us?'

'I wonder if it's something to do with our parents, whoever they are or were? Hey, what if they were with the rebels that old Solon was talking about, and our lives were too much in danger, or something?'

'That would make sense,' said Polly. 'But if it's true, where would our parents be now?'

After much discussion, the two girls decided that the only way to find out was to get away from Petruvio and explore by themselves. Perhaps, on their own, they might enter some of the forbidden areas in Fortuna, and find some useful information. But they were going to have to be very careful. It was difficult to leave their apartment without Petruvio because there always seemed to be guards watching their front door, so they decided to try to lose him when they were already out with him.

They kept a lookout for opportunities and finally, late one afternoon a week or so later, their chance came. As they were strolling back from swimming in a large pool near the edge of Fortuna City, they noticed that Petruvio had stopped behind and was talking to one of the guards. Lisa quickly dragged Polly into a side alley and together they ran down it as fast as they could. At the end of the alley was a canal, flowing swiftly in a westerly direction. They took running dives into the swimway and let the current take them away from the centre of the city. So as to confuse anyone who might have been following them, they dropped on to another canal that was heading north. This they stayed with until all the really large buildings were out of sight. Neither had any idea where they were going – they just knew they were going in a direction they had never been in before, and they were glad to be free of Petruvio's constant watching eye.

After about an hour, they noticed that the canal was running towards some sort of checkpoint in the distance.

Beyond it they could see a line of dingy, single-storey buildings. At the corner of every block were tall towers. They guessed they must be watchtowers because of the uniformed guards they could just make out on the top of each one. At this point, Polly and Lisa slid out of the water and dashed to the cover of a small hut.

The sight that greeted them, as they crept round behind the hut, gave them the first clue as to what Fortuna was really about.

In contrast to the beautiful, affluent people of the city, they saw hundreds of men, women and children, wearing little more than filthy, tattered rags, trudging in long dismal columns that stretched into the distance. Every twenty metres or so were more armed guards shouting and prodding them to walk faster. From their hiding place, the girls studied the sad, hard, defeated expressions on these people's filthy faces as they emerged from tunnels that obviously led underground. The guards on the watchtowers were standing poised with what looked like guns, so nobody could run away – not that any of them seemed capable of such a thing.

'Who are these people?' whispered Lisa. 'Why has no one ever mentioned them?'

'They must be prisoners. Could they be the poor devils who have to do all the work to keep the others in luxury?' whispered Polly. 'Didn't we say this place was all too good to be true?'

After a few minutes Polly and Lisa had seen quite enough and with heavy hearts tracked their way back to a canal that was flowing south. They knew it would be dark-time at any minute and they had to get back to the city before the light went out.

'How many people have to live like that, do you think?' asked Polly when they were safely on their way.

'I don't know, but there were loads of them there. One thing's for sure – you can bet Solon didn't plan on us seeing them.'

'That's it!' cried Polly. 'Don't you see? That's why the guards allow them out at dark-time. They don't want anyone to see them.'

'This must be the big secret – the one we've been trying to uncover. Could it be that anyone who misbehaves or says anything against the leaders "disappears" and becomes a slave like them?'

'Now I'm surprised they didn't make you and me into slaves. Hang on, maybe that's what Solon meant when he threatened us,' said Polly thoughtfully.

Lisa looked all around. They were back in the city now, and surrounded by stately buildings. She spoke very quietly. 'All I know is, we'd better keep our mouths shut when we get back. You remember you once asked me if I was scared. Well, I wasn't then, but I *so* am now.'

Polly shook visibly. 'Me too.'

Although the dark-time siren had not yet sounded,

as soon as they got within a few miles of their apartment, they found themselves surrounded by guards who grabbed them and tied their hands behind their backs. Petruvio must have raised the alarm and it appeared that there had been a wide and frantic search. It was the first time they had been handled roughly, and the first time they knew for sure that they were prisoners in all but word.

That night, their hands were untied and the girls were taken by guards to Solon.

'You have disobeyed me once more,' he said, with a vicious sneer that twisted his whole face. 'I think you should be aware that I am not someone to be trifled with. Normally I would give no second chances. What do you have to say for yourselves?'

Polly spoke up, her voice trembling. 'Sorry, but we got lost. One minute Petruvio was behind us and the next he wasn't.'

'Where did you go for so long?' he rasped. 'What did you see?'

'Nothing, sir, we just travelled round Fortuna on boats.'

The old man stared at each of them with his steely, hawk-like eyes. The two girls both knew that he knew they were lying.

'I am going to break a rule and give you one very last

chance. If you misbehave in any way at all from now on, you will be dealt with accordingly. Now, for the very last time, do you understand what I am saying?'

Polly and Lisa simply nodded and then they were led away by guards.

Petruvio, too, was furious with them. They wondered if he had got into trouble with his uncle for losing them. They promised him faithfully that it wouldn't happen again, but his angry face showed that he didn't really believe them. From that point on there was a strained silence between them.

Eventually, the time came for the Fortuna Aquagames. Practically everyone in Fortuna took part. They divided the races and competitions into categories according to age – although Polly and Lisa had both realised that there was nobody old there. Something else suddenly dawned on them too: all the youngsters were only children – they had no brothers or sisters. When they asked Petruvio, he simply told them that it was the law and the girls now knew better than to try to discuss it further.

The pool in which the competitions took place was stunning – nothing the girls had seen on earth came near it, and both of them had been to a huge number of pools. It was like a huge, oblong, liquid running track, surrounded by countless tiers of seats where the audience sat. This watery track meant that races could be of any distance without the need for the competitors to have to turn round at each end as in normal pools. The starting blocks were lowered on a swing bridge at the beginning of a race and swung back again to create the finish. In the centre was a deep pool where the diving competitions took place.

Polly and Lisa had wondered if anyone would suggest they took part, although they realised in a society in which swimming was part of everyday life, they would stand little chance of winning. Besides, the girls were still in disgrace – Solon would surely not allow them to compete. Luckily, nobody asked them if they wanted to.

The games marked a day of great excitement in Fortuna. Lisa and Polly found themselves surrounded by thousands of citizens, all cheering and waving flags from the stands. The competitors themselves wore much skimpier costumes than the everyday ones and because of this Lisa made a startling discovery.

'Hey, Poll, I've just thought of something,' Lisa whispered urgently. 'Wouldn't you expect everybody to have a little fish symbol on their back, like we do?'

'Of course – I just assumed they did, why?'

'Just look around. We can check now – they're wearing backless costumes.'

Polly looked at the competitors and her mouth fell open. Nobody appeared to have the mark.

'So why do *we* have them then?' she whispered back.

'Do you think it has something to do with the fact that we were taken away from Fortuna, for whatever reason?'

Just as she had finished speaking, Polly noticed that Petruvio was watching them like a hawk. 'I think Petruvio's realised we've spotted something.'

Lisa laughed out loud. 'Best of luck to him. There's not much he can do about it now.'

The girls couldn't help feeling excited as the swimming races got underway. The young people of Fortuna were far and away better swimmers than they had ever come up against at home, and Polly and Lisa found themselves itching to race too.

It was just as the medals and trophies were about to be presented that a girl, a few years older than them, sidled up to where they were sitting. Petruvio was facing the other way, talking to another member of the Imperial household. The girl spoke to them softly and urgently. Her hair was longer than average and she had huge grey-green eyes – she reminded both Polly and Lisa of someone, though neither could think who it was.

'Don't look at me, or act differently. You are in great danger. I know exactly where you come from. We must meet. Come to the woodland area in two days' time.' With that, the girl disappeared into the crowd.

Neither Polly nor Lisa had heard of the woodland area and realised they'd have to take another look at the map of Fortuna in their apartment. They spent the remainder of the afternoon keeping an eye out for the girl, but she seemed to have disappeared as mysteriously as she had appeared.

Chapter 14

POLLY AND LISA COULD do no more than stay in
their apartment, hoping to hear more from the strange
girl about the exact time and place they were to meet
her. They had located the woodlands on the map – it
was on western edge of the dome and was marked,
Timber Area. When no message came from the girl,
they realised that they had to go there anyway and just
hope they met up with her somehow. As Petruvio
would insist on coming with them during the day, and
as it would be very difficult and very dangerous to lose
him again, they knew they would have to leave at night.

Just recently the girls had noticed that the door to
their apartment had remained unlocked overnight.
They assumed this was because they seemed resigned,
even happy, to stay in Fortuna. They had decided to play
at being good girls for a while now, and their strategy

seemed to have paid off. Their door was still guarded, but they thought it would be easier to slip past the guards than lose Petruvio again.

That night, Polly and Lisa opened the door a crack and waited for their chance to escape. The guards remained firmly in position for what seemed like hours. But suddenly there was a loud crash and splashing noise from outside the building, and after consulting each other, the guards rushed away. This was Polly and Lisa's chance, and they managed to escape. It was the first time they had ever been out after dark and they were very frightened. The wide passages with their huge statues and gargoyles that had seemed pretty harmless in the day, were nothing short of menacing in the dark.

They managed to leave the apartment building without encountering anyone. Luckily, they now knew Fortuna quite well and made for one of the main canals heading west. There were a couple of boats that had been left at the stop-off point and the two friends travelled on this canal for quite a time, and were surprised to see no guards on their way. Eventually, they could just make out a line of trees, silhouetted in the distance, way over to the right. They waited until their canal crossed another and dropped down so as to head in that direction. As they drifted into the cover of the forest, they thought they heard a sound – as if someone was paddling along the swimway behind them. Lisa pulled the boat over and waited, hoping against hope that it was the girl from the Aquagames.

As the person climbed out of the water, they saw immediately that it was her, and when she had shaken herself dry, she silently beckoned for them to follow her into the dense cover of the trees. On reaching a tiny clearing, she stopped, turned, and threw them the faintest smile.

'I am sorry to have approached you in such an odd manner,' she said quietly, 'but there was no other way. The woodlands provide good cover, and this part is not being used at the moment. My name is Lydia. I have followed you from the city. I have been waiting there all day. In the end I had to distract the guards so you could slip out. I made sure nobody else followed. You did very well.'

'We're so glad to see you,' said Polly. 'Maybe you can help us.'

Lydia nodded and spoke again in her strange, rather formal manner.

'First, I know that you are telling the truth when you say you come from up above. I have been sent from the Southern Quarter to find you and to persuade you to come back with me. I know that you want to return home.'

Both Polly and Lisa were enormously relieved to hear this and nodded quickly.

'Is there anything you want to ask?' said Lydia.

'We have so many questions,' said Lisa. 'Do you know why we were taken away from Fortuna as babies?'

'I can't answer that exactly,' said Lydia. 'For some reason, you were not supposed to be born. Removing you from Fortuna saved your lives.'

'What do you mean?' asked Polly.

'In order to have a child here, you must apply to the authorities. Usually only those with enough merits or who are highborn are given permission. And no one is allowed to have more than one child. Many people of my age do not even know that women are capable of having more than one. If you *do* have more, or you have one when you are not eligible, it is taken away from you and usually destroyed. Fortuna cannot support a large population, and the governing body want to make sure that only law-abiding people have children.'

'And why aren't there are any old people?' demanded Lisa.

'When you reach the age of sixty years, you are taken away and never seen again. That is just the way it is. It is for the same reason – overpopulation. If they let people live too long, there would be too many and we would all die from lack of air and starvation. That is what we're told, anyway.'

'Don't they mind, these old people?' asked Lisa, horrified.

'The Fortunans are strange. Most people are so brainwashed, they seem to accept their lot without question.'

'So what about the Imperial Governor, Solon? He must be over *seventy* – he looks ancient.'

Lydia smiled sadly. 'If you belong to the ruling class, or earn sufficient merits in your life, you may be permitted to live longer. Very few manage that.'

'But that's terrible! That certainly doesn't happen where we come from,' said Polly.

'But doesn't it get overcrowded?'

'Yeah, 'course, but our world is a huge, huge place with millions of people. Some places get a bit overcrowded, but old people are allowed to live!'

Lydia spoke wistfully. 'The Fortunans are told from when they are little that there is no other world. We are all prisoners here, even if some of us don't realise it. All the ports are heavily guarded and besides that there is no way anyone could ever swim from here now, because the water pressure would crush them.'

Polly took a deep breath and asked the question that had been on her and Lisa's minds since they arrived. 'So how did we get to the surface when we were little?'

Lydia looked all around and her voice dropped to a whisper. 'That I do know. There is a woman, now very old, who rescued as many babies as she could. While some could be hidden in the Southern Quarter, she arranged for others to be taken by one of the fishing boats to the surface. I met her once, I have been told, when I was very young. Few people know her name, or which boat she used, or even exactly where she lives.'

Polly and Lisa could hardly contain their excitement. 'How would we know if we were one of these children?' said Lisa.

'Apparently they were all stamped with a tiny indelible secret mark that contains a number. The parents are given this number in case they are reunited.'

'How can you see the number?' asked Polly excitedly.

'I'm not sure. Do you have this mark?'

'We sure do,' said Lisa, almost proudly. 'Does this mean our parents are here somewhere?'

'I doubt it, but maybe. I really hope so.'

'How do you know all this?'

Lydia looked all around and dropped her voice again. 'Everyone in the Southern Quarter knows about this woman, even if they don't know who or where she is. She is a hero.'

'And why are you helping us?' asked Lisa.

'I once had a twin brother and he too was sent up to the surface. I want to find him – he is my only family now. When the authorities found out about him my parents were sent away, to Devilla.' Poor Lydia shuddered visibly as she spoke the word. 'I should have gone too, but there was a change of plan. I was sent instead to Fortuna – to a horrible family. I later escaped to the Southern Quarter. I would do anything to find my brother, and when you return to the surface, I want to go with you. This is why the people in the Southern Quarter chose me to come and find you. That, and because I am good at moving around unnoticed – unlike most people in the Southern Quarter, I have the same colouring as people in Fortuna.'

'What is Devilla?' asked Lisa.

Lydia suddenly looked terrified. 'I can hardly say the word. Anyone who breaks our laws – like having a child when they haven't got permission, or speaking against our leaders, or even just asking too many questions – can be sent there. It is a huge underground prison, like a city, deep under Fortuna. It is a very dreadful place, so they say, where men, women and children are kept as slaves in abject misery. It is where all our silver and gold and precious stones come from and where our energy systems are maintained. The people work in the factories and fields. They arrive by tunnels from underground. I've heard they are kept like animals.'

Polly looked very sad. 'I think we accidentally came across them, in the north of Fortuna. Those poor people – how do they survive like that?'

'There are thousands of them,' Lydia continued. 'Fortuna is bearable only if you fit in. I mean, have you ever seen any old, sick or injured people, or even people who are not green-eyed and beautiful?'

The girls admitted that they hadn't.

'Anyone different is either destroyed or sent below. Any rebellion is crushed by the polizia immediately.'

'Are they the guards we've seen?' asked Lisa.

'Yes, some of them are guards. Then there are the main polizia who usually go around in such numbers that no one can stand up to them. But at least you can recognise these ones. There are also the secret polizia who dress like ordinary people and listen in to conversations.'

'Why weren't we sent to Devilla or destroyed?' asked Polly, her voice trembling.

'Everyone in the Southern Quarter wonders why too. They have come to the conclusion that Solon must want you both for something. They think there can be only one possible explanation – that you would lead the authorities to the person who saved the babies.'

Polly suddenly felt very scared and even Lisa's face was white with fear.

Lydia took a deep breath and continued. 'The whole system is falling apart. It is ruled by a few old men who think their power will be gone if their subjects begin to believe there is another way of living. You are proof that there is a whole other world out there – so you are very dangerous. Whatever Solon's motives in keeping you alive, he is playing a risky game. That is why it is important that you escape – and, hopefully, help us too.'

'You are so brave to be telling us all this,' said Polly, putting her hand on Lydia's shoulder.

'It seems like the only chance we have of escaping is to find this woman,' said Lisa.

'But how can we do that?' asked Polly.

Lydia hesitated. 'I don't quite know. But she lives somewhere in the Southern Quarter. If I take you there, she may make contact with you.'

'What really goes on in the Southern Quarter?' asked Polly. 'We've heard people talking about it, but we didn't dare ask questions.'

'It's an eerie, neglected place from the outside, but it is not all it appears,' replied Lydia. 'It's not a very large area, but it's where all the people who can't or won't fit in have fled. The people who rule Fortuna have no idea how many of us live there, but there must be many hundreds. The polizia sometimes try to raid it, but they never stay for long. It is a labyrinth of decrepit-looking buildings and only those who live there can find their way round. The woman you seek has been very clever to avoid being found out and tracked down.'

'What's her name?' asked Polly.

Lydia went silent for a second. 'It's funny, but I can't quite remember. It's somewhere in the back of my mind. I seem to recall it being mentioned a lot when I was very little – I just wish I could get it. It was something like Marbelia or Matricia.

Lisa and Polly exchanged a glance. Their minds were made up.

'The only thing we can do, it seems, is to go to the Southern Quarter and wait,' said Lisa, determinedly.

It was as if her words acted as a signal. Suddenly all the lights came on across Fortuna, and the wail of the siren could be heard in the distance.

'What's happening?' said Polly, looking around in terror at the illuminated trees.

'I don't know,' Lydia replied. 'There must be an emergency.'

'What could it be?' asked Lisa, already beginning to guess.

Lydia was silent for a moment. 'Perhaps they have checked your apartment and found you missing. You are very important to them.'

Polly looked terrified now. 'What do you think they will do to us if they find us?'

'We must try to get to the Southern Quarter immediately,' said Lydia, dodging the question. 'It's the only place you will be safe now.'

Chapter 15

MATT MILLER AND KELLY PETERS had become good friends after just a few meetings. When Kelly was over the initial shock of finding out that she was adopted, she became settled into her new identity pretty easily, not just because she'd always felt different to everyone else and now she knew she'd been right, but also because she had a close connection to a good-looking and famous surfer.

Now they had to find out what had happened to the two girls and the significance of the tiny mark they shared. But that, they both agreed, seemed an almost impossible task.

Kelly had wanted to go to the newspapers with the full story, but Matt, who was more used to publicity and how facts could be twisted, thought that for the time being it was a bad idea. He was convinced nobody would believe them anyway.

'They'll just think we're nutcases or weirdos – or worse. After all, they didn't believe the girls could breathe underwater, and they've closed the case now – to them the girls drowned. I just have this totally inexplicable feeling that Polly and Lisa are still alive. It's a bit like twins are supposed to feel when apart. But the least the papers know about it the better, I say. Certainly at this stage.'

'Do you still think someone might be holding on to them?'

'Anything's possible, but I just can't think why. Nobody's asked for any money – not that *I* know of anyway – so it's not likely to be kidnapping.'

'You don't think a secret society has got them, do you? Like the Cult of the Little Blue Fish, or something freaky like that?'

Matt felt a shiver go through his body. 'I just don't know, Kelly. All I do know is that I haven't a clue what's going on.'

'Perhaps they're just waiting for the right moment,' said Kelly. Then a thought struck her. 'Do you think we should dive around where you last saw your friends?'

'Too dangerous. I've thought about that a lot. But if something awful's happened to them it could just as easily happen to us.'

'Then perhaps we should try to find out what the fish

symbol means – what do you think? Maybe if we find something similar it might give us a clue. I suppose I could try Googling it. D'you agree?'

Matt nodded. 'And there must be books full of stuff like that – you know, symbols and things. I've never done much reading and looking in books, but it might be worth trying.'

'Hey, let me do that. We've got a pretty good library at school and I live only two streets from our town one too. I'll try the Net first, though.'

That evening, on the family's computer, Kelly typed 'fish symbol' into Google. There were lots of relevant sites but the only imagery that came up regularly was the fish shape that she'd sometimes seen on cars driven by Christians. Kelly was pretty sure their symbols were nothing to do with that. She did, however, manage to find out that the symbol of the fish went right back to ancient Roman times, before Christianity, when it had represented love and freedom.

Kelly spent all her free time at school searching the Net, or ploughing through history books in the library. She had saved a picture of Matt's mark on her phone so she could refer to it more easily. She had always been rather good at researching things and set about the project in a professional manner. She started by looking way back into the Roman and the Greek civil-isations, then the Egyptian and even trawled through a book on Vikings, but with no success.

It was in the town library that she finally came across a book called *Strange Stories and Amazing Facts* that had a chapter on a lost land known as Atlantis. She discovered that way, way back before the birth of Christ, there was supposed to have been a legendary country that had disappeared under the sea following a massive volcanic eruption. It was thought to have been by far the most advanced society on earth, particularly in the areas of science and engineering. The people had apparently been especially adept at building harbours and canals. When the volcano that was supposed to have been near the centre of Atlantis erupted, the whole landmass was thought to have disappeared through a mighty crater, never to be seen again. Many experts claimed Atlantis had been situated somewhere near the coast of Greece, but no evidence for this had ever been found.

Though Kelly thought all this fascinating, she could see no clear relevance for her and the others. But just as she was shutting the book, her eye caught something that made her stop in her tracks. There was a small photograph of a section of an ancient Egyptian stone tablet, which apparently made some reference to the lost land of Atlantis. Towards the top, and set amongst the strange writing, was an illustration of a little fish. Not just any little fish, however. This one was identical to the one she had on her phone! She quickly photocopied the page and rushed outside to phone Matt.

'It's probably just coincidence,' said Matt, dismissively.

Kelly felt immediately deflated. 'Oh, come on. It's all we've got to go on. And this really could be where the symbol originated!'

'So you think we have some connection to a place that disappeared thousands of years ago? Mmm, really! I *so* believe that.'

Kelly was now a little annoyed. 'OK, smartalec. *You* try and work it out if you're so clever. I'm just trying to work out what the connection is between us – that's you, me and the two other girls – and this place, Atlantis.'

'So what are we going to do about it?'

'Look, I only found out about the symbol five minutes ago. I think that's awesome enough. Give me a break.'

'Sorry, Kell, you did really well. I think it's wicked what you found out,' Matt said apologetically. 'Now we have to decide what to do with the information.'

Chapter 16

THERE WAS NO TIME to lose. Lydia knew Fortuna very well and because of this the three girls were able to head south by crisscrossing the canals and swimways, avoiding the major thoroughfares. Occasionally, in the distance, they spotted the polizia in their powerful launches, tearing hither and thither.

'They're after someone, that's for sure,' said Lydia, as they peeked over the side of a swimway.

Lisa nodded slowly. 'I don't think there's much doubt who it is, either. I wonder if they'll guess we're making for the Southern Quarter.'

'Seeing as that's where all the rebels live, I wouldn't doubt it. I was sure that's where they thought you would go when you left the apartment. That's why I arranged to meet in the woodlands.'

Just as they were approaching a long line of buildings,

they saw what they were dreading most. A checkpoint had been set up way ahead, on the canal they were on. They couldn't swim back against the current, so they jumped out on to the side and ran back to the edge of another canal heading off to the east. Suddenly they heard shots and realised with horror that it was them who were being fired at. In blind terror they dived over the side into the canal.

After changing direction a couple more times, they came back to the original canal, having successfully bypassed the checkpoint.

'That lot should be behind us now, but there are bound to be others,' said Lydia grimly.

Polly and Lisa were terrified. 'Do you think we should give ourselves up?' Polly asked.

Lydia became very serious. 'If you do, I am certain they will kill you – and me too. If their plan was for you to lead them to the old lady, it did not succeed. You are of no use to them now.'

It took another hour to reach the Southern Quarter, and when they arrived Polly and Lisa were shocked at how different it was from the main city. This part of Fortuna had been well and truly neglected. The buildings, though once magnificent, were in an appalling state of repair due to the constant eroding effects of water, which was cascading down from holes in the dome. The beautifully embellished buildings had, over the years, gained a thick, green coating of algae, giving them a gloomy, unnatural look, like ships submerged for decades, or trees choked by ivy. Worse still, the whole place smelled of decaying vegetation, which Polly and Lisa found extremely unpleasant. Many of the canals that had once crisscrossed the area had been so neglected that the water had long leaked out of them. There was such an air of melancholy about the place that it made Polly and Lisa even more nervous. What kind of people would live here? Would they be dangerous?

And where *were* the people? There was no one to be seen, either in the glassless windows of the buildings, or outside them.

'Are there going to be more guards around here?' Lisa asked Lydia.

'They don't usually come this far in, but perhaps they will this time.'

'Did you say some people *choose* to live here?' asked Polly, surveying the dreary panorama that surrounded them.

'Not many choose to. But the ones that do are some of the cleverest in Fortuna. They'd rather live like rats in a squalid place like this than be a part of what we've just left. They are the people who refuse to conform.'

'Don't the rulers try to make them?'

'The rulers try to get rid of them, but they never

succeed. They tried starving them out at one point, but somehow the people survived by growing their own food and eating the rats.'

'*Rats?*'

'Yes, they're the only animals in Fortuna. There are millions of them here.'

'Yuck – imagine having to eat rats! So do people come in and out of the Southern Quarter?' asked Polly.

'There are usually guards checking the canals, but those who live here seldom want to go into the rest of Fortuna. Most of them would stick out in the crowds – they have different colouring and clothing. I'm one of the few people who can blend in.'

Lisa looked puzzled. 'If the residents here are so clever, why don't they rebel and try and overthrow the authorities?'

'A couple of hundred years ago there was a huge revolt, but it was put down with the most enormous cruelty; all those that weren't killed were sent down to Devilla. The few survivors made for the Southern Quarter which, even then, was falling into disrepair. That's when it all started – when this area became a refuge for non-conformists . . .'

Lydia stopped talking suddenly and pointed at another block on the canal, straight ahead, but much closer this time. Worse still, the guards had seen them and were preparing to fire. Quickly the girls swam to the edge of the canal and were relieved to see another canal not far below, heading straight for the interior of the Southern Quarter.

Without hesitating, Lydia flung herself into the air and plunged down into the water below. Polly and Lydia followed swiftly. The guards were running along the edge of the canal and firing water cannons after the girls. Luckily the stinging jets were only effective for a few centimetres under the water, but the girls could still hear them smacking into the water above.

They surfaced a few hundred metres further down to find themselves surrounded by the huge buildings that made up the heart of the Southern Quarter. There was an eerie silence here, that was suddenly and heart-stoppingly broken.

'Did you hear that?' cried Lisa, 'Engines. Could it be the polizia?'

'It is the polizia,' said Lydia. 'They're the only ones allowed to have engines on their boats. We've got to get off these canals, quickly!'

Sure enough, a patrol boat was powering towards them. 'Look there!' yelled Lisa, pointing in the opposite direction. 'More of them! They're coming towards us.'

They looked round to see another patrol boat heading straight for them.

'We're trapped!' screamed Polly.

Just then there was a shout, and a ladder shot out of

a window in a derelict building nearby, coming to rest on the edge of the canal just by them. They could make out the shape of a man inside the building, beckoning them to cross over. Polly and Lisa looked over the side of the canal and realised they were still hundreds of metres in the air. Lydia didn't hesitate, however, and tripped across the rungs of the ladder as if they were centimetres from the ground.

'C'mon!' she yelled.

The two friends had no choice. If they stayed where they were they would be caught by the polizia. They had to cross the flimsy ladder to an unknown fate. Lisa went first, edging her way on her hands and knees, refusing to look down. Polly followed closely after, well aware that the polizia were getting closer and closer. Just as Polly fell through the open window the polizia began firing massive water cannons through the open window of the building.

Chapter 17

THE THREE TERRIFIED GIRLS slithered across the floor to a small door on the opposite side of the empty room. Powerful jets of water smashed against the far wall, causing the plaster to shatter and fill the air with stinging missiles. They followed their unknown rescuer down a gloomy corridor to a stairwell. After almost tumbling down three flights of stairs, they edged out into the half-light and tiptoed across a precarious, makeshift bridge to another building. Without stopping to look back, they raced down another seven flights and out on to a narrow ledge which overhung a small, fast-flowing canal. Once he'd made sure they were still with him, the man dived in and they all followed. They were taken downstream by the fast current and soon found themselves plummeting down a spiral water-chute that emptied into a large pool, hemmed in by the tall buildings.

Their mysterious saviour swam to the middle of the pool and promptly dived, leaving a tell-tale trail of bubbles. Plunging their heads below the surface, they just saw him disappearing through what looked like a small, underwater doorway. They followed him and eventually floated up to the surface of an indoor pool. When they wiped the water from their eyes, they were astounded by the sight that greeted them.

They were in the middle of a cavernous hall, lit by a thousand candles and surrounded by a sea of faces. What struck Polly and Lisa instantly was that among the crowd were older men and women – and not all of them had blond hair and green eyes. Although their clothes were old and tattered, they looked strangely stylish. As the girls climbed out of the water, there was a tumultuous burst of applause. They were led to a small platform at the far end of the hall, where two men and a woman were sitting in large, throne-like chairs.

One of the men stood up and strode towards them with his arms outstretched. 'Welcome to the Independent Southern Quarter,' he cried. 'My name is Theron. We have been expecting you. We sent Lydia here to find you. She is very brave and so, my dears, are you.' Another cheer of approval rose from the crowd.

He turned to Lydia. 'There has been a lot of activity round here since we heard the sirens. You may have noticed the massive build-up of polizia around the perimeters of the Southern Quarter.'

'How did you know we were in the Southern Quarter?' Lisa asked, bravely.

The man smiled at her. 'Our lookouts have been trailing you since you first arrived on the outskirts. Don't worry, you will be safe here with us.

Lisa coughed nervously. 'Won't the polizia find us here?'

'They never stray from the main canals. They can't negotiate our underground network,' Theron replied.

A chorus of laughter came from the crowd and Polly and Lisa were both struck by the fact that this was the first proper laughter they had heard since they arrived.

He then turned to the young man who had led them to safety. 'This is Balia. He has become an expert in tracking. He was one of the children that they were going to send away, many years ago. We managed to rescue him just in time. Unfortunately, his parents weren't so lucky. They were killed by the polizia.'

Balia was about sixteen or seventeen and uniquely handsome, with long almost-black hair, large brown eyes and a twinkly smile that made the girls' hearts race. He was not unlike Petruvio in all but colouring, but there was a light in his eyes and an expression that implied impish humour. When the young man bowed low before them, Polly and Lisa had to try hard not to giggle or go red.

'Over the years our people have become highly experienced at survival and setting traps. Some of the canals that come into the Southern Quarter end so suddenly that anyone travelling on them would fall over the edge into vast chasms. And if they ever did manage to penetrate our corridors, many are booby-trapped. If you didn't know which ones they were, you'd be in severe peril.'

Everyone cheered, obviously remembering incidents from the past.

'You might think we sound cruel – cheering other people's misfortunes. But you must be aware of how cruel and despotic the regime they serve is. Thousands of people have perished at the polizia's hands over the years – and they were the lucky ones. The rest went to Devilla.'

A murmur of agreement came from the crowd.

'Nobody comes or goes without our knowing,' Theron continued. 'Our spies, who go out at dark-time, told us of your arrival here and we spent a long time trying to find a way of getting to you. There were rumours that you must have come from somewhere else – maybe even a world above. We are sure that such a place exists, and we must dedicate ourselves to communicating our plight to that world, and asking for their help. But Solon is determined to hang on to power and will destroy anything that stands in his way.'

'Including us,' murmured Polly, with a shiver.

Theron put his hand on her shoulder. 'Don't worry, we will do everything we can to protect you and you will find everything you need here. We may be poor but we have learned to grow our food and make almost everything we need because we are forced to be self-sufficient. We have gardens on the tops of all the roofs where we grow fruit and vegetables, and in many of the internal pools in the courtyards we have made fish farms. We who dwell in the Southern Quarter hardly ever go out, and if we do it is generally to maintain our security system. The authorities know there are people living here, but they have no idea how many. If they did, they would no doubt make more of an effort to destroy us for ever. We elders in the Southern Quarter are training our young people, both men and women, for the great struggle ahead.' He then smiled kindly. 'It is a very special day indeed. There is so much we want to know. Please answer this question: is it really true that you come from somewhere above the sea?'

Polly cleared her throat nervously and spoke first. 'Yes, we do.'

An excited murmur travelled round the room.

'There really is another world up there, with thousands and thousands of people?'

'More like millions and millions.'

The man looked shocked at first and then almost relieved, as if she had answered the most important question of his life.

Then he suddenly laughed. 'I'm terribly sorry – you young ladies must be exhausted after your recent experiences. You will go to my quarters now, to rest, and this evening we will have a special celebration at which you will be guests of honour. Perhaps you might tell us more of your world then. As you see there are many of us here now. We have all turned out especially to welcome you.'

As the three girls were taken to Theron's quarters by the young man, Balia, they had time to take in their surroundings. If, when they first arrived, Polly and Lisa had found Fortuna bizarre, this interior was even more peculiar. All the walls and ceilings were covered with brightly coloured paintings. Weird abstract statues were set into alcoves, and as they passed through the corridors, strange but pleasant musical sounds wafted through the open doors. The whole place was like a chaotic, arty fairground. To the girls it was the very opposite to the beautiful but strangely soulless Fortuna they had come to know.

They were eventually shown to a room decorated in strange, colourful murals and draped with old, faded wall-hangings. On the floor were what looked like huge beanbags – large enough to curl up in. Set into the walls were tanks containing some of the most beautiful and exotic fish they had ever seen. On a low table they noticed an array of pretty-coloured drinks in handmade pottery cups. Everything had a feeling of warmth and cosiness – it felt very welcoming.

'These are Theron's private quarters,' said Balia. 'You are very honoured.'

'Who'd have thought the Southern Quarter would be like this, judging from what it looked like on the outside?' whispered Lisa. 'That was so ghastly.'

'You're not kidding,' said Polly, falling into a beanbag. 'How about you, Lydia? Where do you usually live?'

'Not very far from here. Theron is my official guardian. He is a wonderful and brave man.'

The three girls were exhausted and slept for several hours. When they awoke, Lydia could hardly wait to ask them more about the world above.

'Tell me about your people. Do they look like the people of Fortuna?

'Some do,' said Polly, 'but we have all sorts.'

'How do you mean, all sorts?'

'Some people have pale skins, some black skins – and there are lots of shades in between.'

Lydia was silent for a moment, staring incomprehensively at them.

'And do all these people live happily together?'

'Yeah, most of the time,' said Lisa, 'but you can't count on it. It's normally all right in England, where we live, but there are lots of wars and things in other places.'

'Here, we are all supposed to be the same. We are not allowed to be different.'

'Many of our fights are to do with religion. Do you have that problem here? Wars happen because some people believe in one god and some believe in another.' Lisa then tried to explain the whole concept of gods and religion, but Lydia found it difficult to work out how things that were supposed to be good could possibly cause people to hurt one another.

Polly and Lisa then began to talk about everyday life above and Lydia's sparkling green eyes opened wider and wider. Nothing could have prepared the poor girl for the world that Polly and Lisa described. Cars, planes, computers and televisions were hard enough for her to understand, but when they started to describe space travel, she became totally confused.

'The sky is something you don't have down here,' said Polly. 'Your world sort of stops at the glass walls of the dome.'

'So where does yours stop then?'

The two friends looked at each other and groaned inwardly. Lisa tried to explain.

'It doesn't,' she said.

'I'm sorry, but how do you mean it doesn't? Surely everything stops somewhere?'

'It's hard to find the right words. We have this thing called a universe that goes on for ever. In a way it's your universe too.'

Lydia looked bewildered. She found it difficult to imagine anything much larger than the dome she lived in, let alone a sky that went on for ever. 'You mean, it's like the sea?' she asked.

'Well, sort of,' said Polly.

'Do you ever go out in this universe?'

Lisa laughed as she realised how limited the world's space programme had really been. 'Not a lot,' she said.

They moved on to mobile phones, which really caught Lydia's imagination.

'Are you telling me you can talk to anyone wherever you are?'

'Yeah – more or less. And you can send written messages if you want, called texts. Oh yeah, and you can take pictures of your friends and . . . '

At this point, somewhat to Polly and Lisa's relief, Balia returned to take them to the banquet. First he led them through to another room where some clothes had been laid out for them. The outfits were very different to anything Polly and Lisa had ever worn before. They were loose and floaty, but eccentric – in keeping with the style of the Southern Quarter. When they were ready, Balia took them through another network of bizarre corridors to a huge room where tables were laid out for what looked like a feast. Every single plate, chair, glass, candlestick and bowl was unique and hand-made, and the whole place had the air of a carnival. As they entered, they were met by another barrage of applause. This time the three girls rather enjoyed the attention and bowed to the assembled crowd.

The meal was to be the finest they had eaten since arriving in Fortuna, and they realised that the people of the Southern Quarter must have sacrificed a great deal to put it on. Best of all for Polly and Lisa was that some of the dishes actually resembled the food they liked at home. There was one that was even a fair competitor to their favourite hamburgers.

'They're probably rat-burgers,' giggled Lisa, only to be dug in the ribs by Polly. Later, it turned out that they were exactly that.

The whole meal was accompanied by a strange, dark, wine-like drink that made them feel very warm inside. Lisa swore that it was alcoholic, even though Lydia had never heard of alcohol.

When they had all finished eating, Polly and Lisa were called upon to speak of the world above. Normally they would have been rather shy in front of so many people – even Lisa – but whether it was the strange drink, the friendliness and interest of the audience, or their delight at finally being allowed to speak of their previous lives, they found they were able to talk non-stop.

Right at the end of their tales, Polly mentioned the mysterious woman who had arranged to send them to the surface all those years ago. She said that they had been told she might live in the Southern Quarter. 'We want to find her, and see if she can take us home.'

There were quiet whispers. Eventually Theron, Lydia's guardian, spoke. 'I'm sorry, young ladies, but I'm afraid we cannot help. Apart from Lydia I know of no one who has ever met this person. No one even knew that she had been successful – until you arrived.'

Polly and Lisa exchanged helpless glances. Were they ever going to be able to leave Fortuna?

Chapter 18

PROFESSOR CHRIS BUCKLEY OF Cambridge University was sitting in his study, staring out of the window at the students in the quadrangle below. But his mind was on other things. Although relatively young, he was one of Britain's leading experts on ancient civilisations and he was feeling distinctly excited. The night before he had been a guest on a programme about Ancient Greece on BBC2, in which he had mentioned Atlantis. That morning he had received a phone call from a young man who had seen him. The boy's name was familiar – he had read about him in the paper a couple of months back.

It was an odd story, he recalled. Two young girls had gone missing at sea. They had dived off a boat, claiming they could breathe underwater, and then simply disappeared without trace. The press had been full of theories about the dangerous waters where they had gone missing, and many of the locals had claimed that there were mysterious creatures down below. No trace of the girls' bodies had been found and the main suspect, the boy who had just phoned, had been released due to insufficient evidence. The professor remembered hesitating over the article at the time, and feeling a strange, inexplicable tingle of excitement.

Most of Professor Buckley's life since he had been a student had been spent studying lost civilisations, particularly those that had disappeared beneath the sea. He was convinced that the most well-known, the lost world of Atlantis, must have existed, despite current thinking that it was just a myth that had become exaggerated over the centuries. For the last few summers he had chartered fishing boats and trailed up and down the coastlines of Greece and Turkey with his wife, Susan, searching in vain for just one clue that might lead him to its precise location.

Up to now, despite having come across nothing solid to back up his theories, his tireless studies in libraries all over the world had led him to the conviction that somewhere down there were the remains of cities and forests and some of the most wonderful art that had ever been produced. Now this boy had told him that he had some evidence linking the modern world to a civilisation that had flourished several thousands of years ago.

Matt Miller was just about to leave for Australia for the surfing championship, so there was no time to waste. Professor Buckley had arranged to meet him, along with a girl who was somehow involved, in a café in Abingdon that Saturday.

Matt told the professor the whole story, from when Lisa and Polly had first approached him; to their discovery of a shared birthmark, ability to breathe underwater, and that all three had been abandoned babies. Then Kelly confirmed that she too shared these attributes, and showed him the photo of the mark on their backs and the photocopy of the symbol from the library book.

'But this is quite astonishing,' said the professor. 'Why should there be references to Atlantis – if it *is* Atlantis – on an Egyptian parchment? I must have missed that. But you're right, these images are too similar to be coincidental. And you really claim you can all breathe underwater?'

Matt laughed. 'Look, I didn't think I could until Kelly showed me how. It's really spooky, to tell the truth.'

'But it's physically impossible for human beings to extract oxygen from the water. We just haven't evolved in that way.'

Matt shrugged. 'That's why we haven't told anyone,

except you, now. We think we must be some sort of freaks.'

'How exactly do you do it?'

Kelly explained about the click in her head when she had first tried to force water quickly through her nose.

Professor Buckley looked throughtful. 'It almost sounds as if you have some extra feature in your respiratory system that simply had to be given a kick-start. Something we other mere mortals don't have. Have you any objections to being examined by one of my medical friends? I promise it will be done in secret. This is far too important to leak out in dribs and drabs.'

Matt looked serious. 'All I really care about at this stage is finding out what happened to Lisa and Polly. So you do believe us?'

The professor smiled. 'Let's put it this way: I cannot think of any reason whatsoever why you two should make it up. You obviously aren't trying to make money out of it. If what you are telling me is even partly true, it will rock the medical, historical and geographical worlds to their foundations.'

'So what do you want us to do now?' asked Matt.

'You go off to Australia as planned, Matt, and I will stay in touch with you, Kelly, if that's all right? I won't do anything without your complete agreement. All I can do is thank you for contacting me. I feel very honoured.'

Chapter 19

Despite reports from the lookouts in the
Southern Quarter on the frantic movements of the
polizia, Polly and Lisa managed to spend a few fairly
stress-free days there. They met Lydia's friends, who
turned out to be everything the other young people in
Fortuna hadn't been: they were open, friendly and
inquisitive, and fascinated by what Polly and Lisa had
to say about where they came from. When the two
friends had first realised that life in the Southern
Quarter was spent continually indoors, they had found
the whole idea unbelievably depressing. They now
realised that the people who lived there had little choice
– the only way they could protect themselves was by
staying deep within the cover of the buildings.

The brightest side to the whole experience came
when they visited the superb greenhouses that had been

built into the roofs of the otherwise austere buildings. The clever scientists of the Southern Quarter had developed a unique system involving the use of large magnifying glasses and mirrors which increased the light available thousands of times. These lenses bathed the whole place in warmth. The spray from the leaking glass dome-panels, though depressing from the outside, gave the greenhouses a tropical rainforest feel and they were full of luscious plants and colourful birds – the only ones the girls had ever seen in Fortuna. Most of the plants and trees were covered in all sorts of delicious exotic fruit that the girls had never seen before. Their favourite was one that looked like a red pear and tasted similar to strawberry ice cream.

The rooftop greenhouses were connected by narrow, covered walkways that could hardly be seen from down below due to the heavy, swirling mist created by falling droplets. Polly and Lisa loved being able to walk around freely without the nagging sensation that they were continually being spied on.

When a week had passed, however, they began to feel frustrated and claustrophobic again. In a way, Polly and Lisa felt they were just as much in prison here as they had been before. Would they ever find the person they were looking for – the person who might get them back home?

Suddenly it all changed.

Polly, Lisa and Lydia were walking through one of the gardens on their way to meet a group of their new friends, when a small, dark-haired boy rushed up to Lydia from nowhere and pushed a slip of paper into her hand. He stood under one of the taller bushes a few metres away, as if waiting for her reaction. On the paper was a sketch of the small fish that they knew so well, and the word 'Maricia'.

'This is it!' cried Lydia. 'This is what we've been waiting for – I'm absolutely sure of it. This is the name of the woman I met when I was little.'

'I think he wants us to follow him,' whispered Polly, putting her finger to her lips and carefully checking that nobody around was watching.

'Try not to make it too obvious,' said Lydia. 'We know that there are spies about, maybe even here.'

'How do we know *he's* not a spy?' asked Polly.

'We don't – but it may be our only chance,' Lydia replied.

The boy darted in and out of the trees and shrubs, making it difficult to follow him. But follow him they did – from rooftop garden to rooftop garden, over rickety bridges hundreds of metres above the ground, and then through a tiny doorway and down a narrow, winding staircase. Down and down they went until, after descending countless steps and feeling dizzy and dis- orientated, they reached ground level. The girls stepped outside the doorway gingerly and surveyed what was probably the dreariest landscape they had ever set eyes on. There was not a plant or a tree or a blade of grass – let alone a person – anywhere: just rocks and rubble and huge, dirty puddles with clusters of dishevelled rats staring at them inquisitively. A slow drizzle completed the sad picture. The boy noticed his followers become hesitant and urged them to continue by beckoning frantically. They walked on and on between the decrepit buildings until eventually they had travelled so far that they found themselves approaching the very southern perimeter of the dome.

One minute the boy was standing right in front of them waving, and the next minute he was gone. They ran forward and came across what looked like an oversized rabbit hole with a narrow staircase leading downwards. Now they were going *below* ground level!

The staircase was lit by tiny rush candles and opened into a vast vaulted hallway like the crypt of an ancient monastery. The little boy disappeared into one of a number of passageways and the three girls did their best to follow. After passing more doors than they could count, they came across one that was ajar.

Lisa turned to look at the other two. 'Shall we go in?' she asked, nervously. Polly and Lydia, sensing that their quest was almost over, nodded with determination. Together, the three girls entered the room.

Inside, in a cosy little apartment full of pictures of smiling children, rocking gently in a chair by an open fire, was perhaps the oldest lady they had ever seen.

'Welcome, my dears,' the old lady said in a quiet, slightly breathless voice. 'My name is Maricia and I have been waiting for you. My spies tell me you two came from the land above and I wanted to meet you. You are the first of my children to return and you are so very, very welcome. I never knew until now whether any of you had survived or not. Please come nearer the light so that I may look at you more closely.'

Polly and Lisa stepped forward nervously, leaving Lydia in the shadows, as the old woman chuckled with happiness.

'What fine young ladies you have become, to be sure! It makes me very proud. Now, how much do you know about me?'

Lisa spoke first. 'We don't know very much, except you must be the lady who arranged for us to go to the surface when we were babies. You saved our lives.'

'It is a very long story, but I will try to tell you what happened. You have met Solon, I believe. Solon may seem wise and kind, but kind he most certainly is not. He is the latest in a long line of cruel, vicious dictators who have ruled with an iron fist. Solon rewards his polizia well, but anyone who disagrees with him is sent to Devilla. Have you heard of Devilla?'

Lisa and Polly nodded.

'It is a terrible, terrible place. My husband discovered the way out to the upper ocean many, many years ago. Up to that time, we had only known about the gap through which you must have entered and the pressure of the water rushing in from above made it impossible to go upwards that way. My husband was a fisherman and he was out fishing one day when he discovered another narrow gap in the rock ceiling, hidden by heavy weed. This tiny gap led through to the upper world. At that time, many babies were either being destroyed or sent to Devilla with their parents for a life of slavery. We decided we must try to help. We managed to hide some babies in the Southern Quarter, but we feared for their safety, and so we had the idea to take them up to a different world. Parents would come to me with their newborn babies, and I would look after them secretly until my husband was able to make the trip. He would leave his fishing boat close to the gap, and then, carrying each baby in a special sling on his back he squeezed up through the gap until he reached the upper ocean. He then swam long distances to find safe beaches on which to leave them. He was the most magnificent swimmer – at one stage he was the champion of all Fortuna. We saved many, many babies this way. But then the authorities got suspicious and we decided we must move here to escape the polizia.'

'Couldn't you have escaped too?'

'Maybe we *all* should have escaped, my dear, but we wanted to help save babies – and Fortuna is our home, after all. It was a decision that was to become a life sentence. A few years ago, the authorities came near to discovering us. Since then we have had to stop.'

'How many children have you saved altogether?' asked Lydia.

The old lady picked up a leather-bound book and thumbed through to the back. 'Let me see . . . to date it must be about twenty-five. My late husband and more recently my son have put them down in many places along the coast. Until you came along, we had no idea whether any of you had actually survived.'

'Can you tell us who our parents are?' asked Polly.

The old lady sighed deeply. 'I hope so, my dears. You both have your mark, I take it?'

'Is it in the shape of a fish?'

'Yes, the emblem of Fortuna. I stamped it on your backs when you were taken away. Come over here – I must look at the number on them.'

Polly wasn't sure what she meant, but she walked over and lifted her shirt. The old lady scrabbled around in a drawer and took out a strange-looking contraption, like a cross between a magnifying glass and a microscope.

'My great-grandson, Pietro, will have to examine them – I am nearly blind these days. Come over to the light, Pietro, darling.'

The boy, suddenly appearing in the doorway, walked over and peered through the eye-piece.

'What do you see?' asked the old lady.

'I see a number, Great Grandmother. There's a one and a seven.'

Maricia began to thumb through the pages of the book.

'Now let me see. Ah yes, seventeen, that was in our year one thousand and five. It says here that your mother and father were called Oliviera and Aurelius. You were named Theodora.'

Despite the seriousness of the situation, Lisa dug Polly in the side and began to laugh. 'I bet you're glad that got changed!'

'Let's wait to see what yours is,' muttered Polly tetchily. 'Do you know what happened to them?' she asked urgently, turning back to the old lady.

'They were sent down to Devilla, my dear. I am so terribly sorry.'

'Please, please, could you look at mine now?' said Lisa, suddenly desperate to find out her own identity.

The little boy put the contraption to Lisa's back. 'There is a two and a one, Great Grandmother.'

The old lady consulted her book once again.

'Twenty-one. It says here that your mother was called Delinia and your father Fredorius. I regret to say they too were sent to Devilla for having a second child.'

'Will they still be alive?' asked Lisa, on the verge of tears now.

'Unfortunately, my dear, we have no way of knowing. We believe that many people perish in Devilla because of the severity of the life they are forced to endure.'

Lisa burst into huge sobs and Polly put her arms round her. She had never seen the confident, happy-go-lucky Lisa like this before. 'But it's my fault,' Lisa said, through her tears. 'If they hadn't had me, they'd have been all right.'

'Come on, Lisa,' Polly whispered. 'Somehow we're going to find out whether our real mums and dads are still alive and then we're going to rescue them, even if we have to devote our lives to it.'

The old lady looked grave. 'I'm afraid that no one has ever managed to rescue anyone from Devilla – nor has anyone escaped.'

'We'll see about that,' said Lisa, suddenly looking as if she could kill. 'Let them try and stop us!' Then she paused, and her expression changed to a curious one. 'By the way, what was *my* name?'

'It says here that you were called Hortensia.'

Polly tried her best not to laugh, but even Lisa saw the funny side, and they both fell into a fit of the giggles.

'My parents are in Devilla too,' announced Lydia, stepping forward.

'I believe I know that, my dear. Your name is Lydia, isn't it? We met when you were very young. You are an exceedingly brave girl. I have heard all about what you have done and I am very honoured to meet you again. Your parents were indeed sent to Devilla, but we managed to claim that you were the only child of a couple who died of the fever. That was how you were saved. It is all here in my little book.'

Lydia spoke again. 'Would you be able to tell me the number of my brother? He was taken away when I was tiny.'

'I remember, my dear. I remember you as a baby, at the time when your parents brought your brother to me. I made a special note. Now let me see. Ah yes, here it is. I believe he was number fourteen. His name was Antonio.'

Lydia looked relieved and excited at the same time.

'You have done so much for so many people, and taken big risks. You must be in great danger,' said Lydia, holding the old lady's frail hand in hers.

Maricia laughed gently. 'Oh, that doesn't matter now. I am very, very old and my own life means nothing to me. But I worry about my son; he is far braver than me.'

Polly could contain herself no longer and plucked up courage to ask the big question. 'Would your son take us back to the surface?'

'I don't know if it is possible any more. He hasn't been up for a long time now. He is still a fisherman, but there are patrol boats everywhere, disguised as fishing boats. To make matters worse, they really do fish while they are patrolling, so that even we don't know which is which. Goodness knows what they would do if they found the way out to the world above. They would probably seal it up. For all we know, they might have done so already.'

'What if we were to tell your son that if he can take us home, we will come back to rescue your people?' said Polly firmly. 'We on the surface are very advanced compared to Fortuna in a lot of ways. We could prepare a huge rescue force.' Polly sounded brave and determined, but she hadn't really thought this through. For all she knew, everyone would just laugh at their story.

The old lady looked thoughtful. 'I will have to speak with my son. He hates the way the people here are forced to live and would do anything if he thought there was a chance of changing it – even risk his own life.'

Then they heard a muffled noise outside. 'It sounds like the polizia, Great Grandmother!' the little boy shouted.

Maricia seemed completely unfazed. 'Pietro,' she said calmly, 'shut the door and bolt it, there's a good boy. I expect the entrances to the catacombs have already been sealed. Even if they did get down here, there are maybe a hundred such doors in each passage – it would be hours before they got here. However, you girls must get away. You can leave by the hidden tunnel – just follow young Pietro here. The passage is over there behind that bookcase. You will have to tell me about your world another time. Now you must go. I will speak to you again, soon, I promise. Just keep a lookout for Pietro and do what he asks you to do.'

The three girls kissed the old lady goodbye and ran to the bookcase, which revolved to reveal a dark passageway.

Chapter 20

PROFESSOR CHRIS BUCKLEY HAD hardly slept since speaking to Matt and Kelly in the café. His head was full of little blue fish, abandoned babies and youngsters who could breathe underwater. He had arranged for Kelly to be examined at the Radcliffe Hospital in Oxford, where one of his old university friends, Dr Tom Bailey, was head of research. Kelly had told her parents she was going to visit a friend – she hated lying, but she didn't feel able to tell them the truth . . . yet.

Kelly was in Tom Bailey's office with Professor Buckley when the X-rays came back. They crowded round as the doctor pinned them to the light box.

'Take a look at this,' said the doctor, excitedly. 'Have you ever seen anything remotely like it?'

'What's so special about it?' Chris Buckley asked. He sounded disappointed.

Kelly found it a bit unnerving staring at her own skull, but, like Professor Buckley, she could see nothing out of the ordinary.

'Look just behind your ear cavities, Kelly. There are two little shadows that look like tiny valves.'

'Don't we all have those?' asked the professor.

'No. I don't know what they are. Look, I'll be honest, the only time I ever saw anything remotely like them was when I was dissecting fish at medical school – sorry, Kelly. I know it sounds odd, but it looks as if you have internal gills.'

He turned back to the X-ray. 'Have you ever had any surgical work done on your nasal or oral functions, Kelly?'

'Do you mean my nose and ears? No, never. I've only ever been to the doctor once, and that was when I fell off my bike.'

'Chris here told me that when you dive, you take in water through your nose and push it out through your mouth. Is that right?'

'I think some goes out through my ears as well. I'm not quite sure.'

'And this friend of yours, Matt, he's the same?'

'And the girls that went missing,' added Kelly.

Professor Buckley turned from the X-ray. 'For all we know there could be hundreds of people like this. Many of them might not even know they can do it.'

'Where are you taking it from here, Chris?' asked the doctor. 'Because I should really inform the medical papers. What we see here is more significant than any other anatomical discovery in the last hundred years.'

'Sorry, Tom. I know it's an amazing discovery, but I really think we should wait a bit. Imagine how these kids will be hounded by the press if this gets out.'

'Mmm, I suppose you're right. Hang on, there was something else, wasn't there?' the doctor said. 'You mentioned strange birthmarks. Kelly, could we examine yours under our new digital microscope? We're testing it for the manufacturers.'

'You'll never guess what,' the doctor said as he looked at the mark, minutes later. 'Using this microscope, I can see a *number* on the fish. There's absolutely no doubt. Kelly here is number twenty-five – whatever that means!'

Chapter 21

THE THREE GIRLS GOT back to the main building complex of the Southern Quarter to find that everyone was talking about the recent raid by the dreaded polizia. It was one of the biggest in living memory, and although they hadn't managed to break into the main living areas, they had caused extensive damage to the buildings and gardens with their water cannons. Everyone was certain they were looking for the girls.

But instead of resenting the trouble the girls had brought upon the community, everybody was kind and supportive and more determined than ever that they should remain. They even went so far as to put guards on their door at night, just to make sure that they were safe.

It was calm for the next few days, and everyone began to relax. About a week later, however, messengers tore through the corridors, shouting at the tops of their voices that the largest force that had ever been seen was pouring into the Southern Quarter in hundreds of launches.

At the very same moment, Pietro appeared at the doorway to the girls' room. Once again, he beckoned urgently. They were being summoned to return to the old lady. As they raced through the corridors with him, despite their imminent attack, everyone called out to wish them good luck. Just as the girls were approaching the staircase to ground level, they heard a mighty rumble, followed by the sound of running feet. A horde of heavily armed polizia were blocking their path. The ones at the front recognised Polly and Lisa instantly and began to run towards them.

Little Pietro, as cool as ever, turned into an open doorway on the right and slammed the door once they were all through. Then he raced across the room – much to the surprise of the occupants – and leaped through an open window on the far side. The girls could do nothing but follow. They reached the window just as the polizia opened the door. Pietro had tumbled some five metres into a round pool and he motioned for them to come. Polly, Lisa and Lydia hit the surface with three consecutive splashes. They surfaced to see the young boy climbing down a ladder attached to the side of one of the surrounding buildings. When he'd gone down about twenty rungs, he disappeared through another window and again beckoned to them. Poor Lisa had never been very good at heights and, seeing the ladder stretching way down almost a hundred metres to the ground, she felt that she might pass out. She had to be helped on to the top rung by Polly and Lydia, and with closed eyes, managed to scramble down behind the others.

The polizia were now coming at them from all directions with some of them lining up their heavy water cannons to blast them off the ladder. By the time Lydia, who was last, got to the window, one of the polizia had just reached the top of the ladder. When they were all inside, Pietro pulled the most remarkable stunt. On the wall by the window was a lever, which he yanked with all his might. As he did so, the hooks holding the ladder to the outside wall slid away and the ladder swung out drunkenly toppling into the void below, with at least half a dozen of their pursuers clinging to it.

But there was no time to spare. The young boy promptly led them to yet another indoor staircase which spiralled down to ground level.

When the little party eventually reached the old lady, she was waiting anxiously.

'Welcome again, my dears. It seems you are the centre of a great deal of excitement. We must help you to get away immediately – our spies have told us that the order has been sent to terminate you. My dear, brave son has agreed to do another trip. He is waiting for you at the southern port. Somehow, we must get you aboard his boat without attracting any attention. It must look like a routine fishing trip. Are you ready, my dears?'

Polly, still panting from the journey, gasped, 'We're really grateful for all you've done. We promise we will never forget you.'

'Never ever,' said Lisa. 'And we will tell everyone on earth who will listen. One day we will come back, that is a promise.'

'I fear I have not much time left,' wheezed the old lady. 'But that is of no consequence. All that is important is that your world gets to hear of our terrible plight.'

The old lady smiled at the three of them. 'Enough. Go now – and good luck!'

With that, Pietro led the three girls once more through the revolving bookcase at the end of the candlelit room, to embark on their perilous journey.

Chapter 22

THE BOY MOVED SWIFTLY through the dingy corridors, dodging between the crowds of anxious people from the Southern Quarter, fleeing the polizia. Despite the best efforts of the girls, Pietro found himself having to stop every now and again and wait for them to catch up. After about an hour, the three girls realised from the strong smell of fish that they were getting close to the southern fishing port at the outer wall. The boy stopped and ordered them to wait in the shadows while he checked the situation. They were now not far from the port where his grandfather's boat was moored.

After a very tense wait the boy returned with his grandfather – a handsome man, with a craggy face that reminded the girls of his mother, the old lady.

'I am very pleased to meet you,' he said. 'My name is Silas. I have come to take you to the surface.'

'Will it be possible to get away without the polizia capturing us?' asked Lydia anxiously.

The fisherman looked grim. 'It will be hard but we have decided what we will do. We must create a diversion – enough to draw everyone away from the port and distract Solon and his men from looking for you.'

'A diversion like what?' asked Polly.

'I have thought long and hard. I think if there was a power cut, we should be able to get away.'

'A power cut? Total darkness? But how could it be done? It's never happened before,' said Lydia.

'One of our people has access to the main engine rooms that generate power for the lighting network. He is going to sever the huge pipeline to this area. The result should be almost immediate. As soon as the power is cut, we must go to my boat. We must be out of Fortuna before the light comes back on. If we are not, we will be destroyed.'

There was no time to waste – the explosion was due to happen at any moment. Suddenly, Silas was no longer with them. Before they could panic however, they heard a loud rumble from underneath them and the ground shook. The lights flickered for a few seconds and then they were thrown into total darkness. Then they saw a spotlight coming towards them – and to their huge relief, realised that it was the beam of a powerful torch, held by Silas.

A loud siren broke the silence, followed by hysterical shouting from all around. People were running everywhere in blind panic. Even the polizia seemed out of control in the darkness, mingling with the masses in the vain hope that they knew where they were going.

Silas told his grandson and the girls to follow, and with the help of the torch, the little group made their way to the entrance to the port ahead. On a couple of occasions they were actually passed by polizia, who seemed far too distracted to pay them any attention. When they arrived at the port, the guard post was deserted. Nobody noticed as they slid silently through the darkness between the huge boats towards the one that belonged to Silas.

And then they saw the boat, right on the end, by the huge doors that led, eventually, to the lower ocean. As they got closer, Polly and Lisa noticed that the whole of the outside of the boat was covered in thick steel scales like those of a fish, presumably to protect it from the enormous water pressure. The little party crept quickly across the narrow gangplank and through a small metal hatchway that led down into the cabin.

The eerie wail of the siren stopped just as Silas revved the huge motor and began to slide the boat towards the inner gates that led out into the departure area. At that moment, however, emergency lights began to come on around them. The guards were heading back to their posts, too, but hadn't yet noticed that the boat right at the head of the queue was missing.

Their hearts were thudding as Silas edged his boat into the departure area. It was with great relief that the little crew watched the doors closing behind them. Luckily, everything from that point onwards was automatic. Water gushed in from all around and as soon as the chamber was completely full, the massive outer doors began to swing open, allowing the craft to move out slowly into the lower ocean.

They had finally left the dome, and their escape had gone unnoticed! As they looked back, the city of Fortuna, lit by the eerie glow of emergency lighting, looked more dark and menacing than ever.

The submarine gradually built up speed and within half an hour the seemingly endless dome which surrounded Fortuna was becoming just a hazy shape in the distance.

'We've done it!' yelled Lisa, leaping around the small cabin. 'We've finally got free from that ghastly place!'

'Don't celebrate too soon,' cried Silas over the roar of the massive steam engines. 'There is a chance that a guard may have seen our departure and if so, they will certainly send boats after us.'

'Will they be able to catch us?' asked Lydia.

'Their boats are faster than mine. I'm going to turn

off all the lights and try to steer blind from now on – that way it will be more difficult for them to see us, and more difficult for other fishing boats to see us too. I am fairly sure I can steer by the compass.' With that, he turned off the main beam that illuminated a wide arc in front of the boat and then all the cabin lights, leaving just one so that he could read the dials.

Cruising through the lower ocean without lights was the most eerie experience. They were aware from vibrations of huge fish and sea mammals passing them, but they couldn't see them.

'How long before we reach the gap in the ceiling?' shouted Lisa, over the engine noise.

'If we keep up this rate, we should be there within an hour or so,' replied Silas. 'It all depends on whether or not we are intercepted. I think you girls, and you, Pietro, should keep an eye out for anything attempting to follow us.'

At this command, the four of them stationed themselves at different portholes, scanning the water for any other craft.

They travelled in silence for a while, each person deep in their own thoughts.

Polly had been trying to imagine the journey that had happened fourteen years before, when she first made this trip. 'How did you know we would be found when you brought us up as babies?' she asked Silas.

'Sometimes, when we placed babies on the sand, we hung around in the water until someone came along. But other times, we just had to leave the babies, hoping against hope that they would be discovered. Some must have perished. We even left one poor boy on a boat that had somehow broken loose in a storm. I often wonder what happened to him.'

'I believe we might know,' said Lisa proudly. 'His name's Matt Miller and he's now a famous surfer.'

Silas frowned. '*Surfer?* Sorry, I don't know what that is.'

The girls tried to explain the principles of surfing, but poor Silas seemed none the wiser.

'He was the one we left on the surface when we first came down,' added Polly.

As the girls peered through the tiny portholes they saw more weird and wonderful sea creatures drifting by. There was an enormous, almost see-through squid, as large as the boat they were in, with pale, luminous eyes on stalks which followed them lugubriously as they flew past; there was a herd of what looked like giant sea-horses, which would have been big enough to ride in any other circumstances, and scary black manta rays larger than anything that had ever been seen in the seas above, slowly flapping their wings, like grotesque vampires crossing a night sky. But most numerous of all were the shoals of pale, silver fish, doing their best to get out of the way of their major predator which, for once, seemed not to be remotely interested in them.

And then they came to the top of the lower ocean. Stretching as far as the eye could just see above them, with long tendrils of seaweed covering its rocky surface, was the ceiling which separated the ocean they were in from the one above. The submarine slowed down and Silas put the headlights back on. He skilfully moved along the rocky surface, checking his compass readings and searching for anything that might indicate the split leading upwards.

'What's that?' yelled Lisa after about half an hour, pointing out of her porthole.

They all stared, and as they did so, they noticed that a shoal of long, slim fish seemed to be disappearing into the very rock itself about twenty metres ahead. Silas swung the boat slightly to starboard and sure enough, hidden amongst a forest of dark green tendrils, was what looked like a narrow passageway.

'We have no time for long goodbyes,' Silas said grimly. 'I wish you the best of luck. Please don't forget us. Remember, should you want to return, I will pass by the entrance hole every thirty days from today.'

'You will see us again,' said Lisa, close to tears. 'I promise. Thank you for all you have done, Silas. And thank you, too, Pietro.'

The boat slowed to a halt and Silas turned to the

girls with a grim smile. 'This is as far as I can go. At some places the gap is only wide enough to let one person through at a time, let alone a boat like this.' He raised a hand in farewell, as did his grandson, Pietro.

The three girls ran through to the hold at the front of the boat, and Polly and Lisa were reminded of the one that had scooped them up all those months ago. They waited impatiently while it filled with water and the massive jaws began to cantilever open. Then all they had to do was float out into the lower ocean and make their way a few metres towards the dark gap in the rock ceiling.

The swim up through the chasm was not easy. Silas was right – the gap was very narrow and they had to feel their way along. At some points they had to squeeze between sharp rockfaces, trying to avoid scratching their skin or snagging their suits. After about half an hour, however, they noticed a tiny speck of light way up ahead and soon they had reached the warmer, brighter sea above!

When the girls struck the surface they were almost blinded by sunlight. It was a beautiful, clear autumn morning! Polly and Lisa breathed fresh sea air deep into their lungs. It felt wonderful! Lydia, of course, was struck dumb by her first view of the sky.

Lisa noticed a thin, dark line on the horizon in one direction. With renewed energy, the girls made for the

Coming soon

RETURN TO FORTUNA
by g.g. elliot

Polly and Lisa return to the surface, with their
Fortunan friend, Lydia. Although delighted to be
home, they know they must go back to Fortuna, and
they take Kelly and Matt with them.
The Southern Quarter is now in a terrible state.
With their friends there, they come up with a
desperate plan to overthrow the Imperial Governor.
But while Polly and Lisa are captured by the polizia,
Matt and Lydia enter the most terrifying place of all.

Look out for these other Piccadilly Pearls

VENUS SPRING: STUNT GIRL
by Jonny Zucker

Venus Spring is fourteen years old and this is the first
summer she's been allowed to go to stunt camp. It's a
dream come true; something she has been working
towards for years. But while she's there she stumbles
on a devious and terrifying plot that threatens
the surrounding countryside.

'A fast-paced, thrilling read'
The Sunday Times

VENUS SPRING: BODY DOUBLE
by Jonny Zucker

When Venus Spring's friend, DCI Radcliff, hears
rumours that a gang are going to kidnap the child
star, Tatiana Fairfleet, she wants to give Tatiana some
protection without causing panic. So she asks Venus
to act as Tatiana's body double at her boarding school
– providing a decoy if there are any problems.
Venus finds herself caught in real danger.
She must use all her skills to stop events spiralling
out of control.

GIRL WRITER: CASTLES AND CATASTROPHES
by Ros Asquith

Cordelia Arbuthnott wants to write books. Not the sort that her aunt, the bestselling children's author Laura Hunt writes, but literary masterpieces. But writing a masterpiece is trickier than she expected. Real life just keeps getting in the way! Welcome to the wacky, hilarious world of Cordelia. And for readers who are also aspiring writers, there are some fantastic top tips on getting your story right.

HONEYSUCKLE LOVELACE: THE DOG WALKERS' CLUB
by Cherry Whytock

There comes a time in almost everybody's life when they have a brilliant idea. Honeysuckle Lovelace's Brilliant Idea is to set up a Dog Walkers' Club with her friends. The club's first 'client' is Cupid, Mrs Whitely-Grub's poodle. As Cupid becomes a regular, Honeysuckle grows increasingly suspicious of his owner. She's determined to solve the mysteries surrounding Mrs Whitely-Grub – and the Dog Walkers' Club provides the perfect cover!